W9-AUE-061

KNEELING
ON RICE

DATE DUE

KNEELING ON RICE

STORIES

Elizabeth Denton

University of Missouri Press
Columbia and London

Library of Congress Cataloging-in-Publication Data
Denton, Elizabeth.
    Kneeling on rice : stories / by Elizabeth Denton.
        p.   cm.
    Contents: The skinner box — Generations — Kneeling on
rice — Koh Samui — About Johanna — A leap of faith —
Callings — The retreat — A house guest — Man for man —
Bold.
    ISBN 0-8262-0968-8 (pbk. : alk. paper)
    I. Title.
PS3554.E589K64   1994
813'.54—dc20   94-15564
                                                        CIP

©™ This paper meets the requirements of the American
National Standard for Permanence of Paper for Printed
Library Materials, Z39.48, 1984.

Designer: Stephanie Foley
Typesetter: Connell-Zeko Type & Graphics
Printer and binder: Thomson-Shore, Inc.
Typefaces: Klang and Palatino

For Acknowledgments, see page 171.

To Mark

Love makes gratitude feel
weightless, like song

Contents

KNEELING ON RICE

The Skinner Box

1.

He'd been disappointed in love, the young Chinese woman peering in the window of her teacher's home knew. She spied on him openly at first, her nose just touching the dirty glass. Looking, she wondered how his face—the face of a white American—could look so severe and troubled. Had his society mistreated him? Westerners whine about their parents, she remembered. Had they been cruel to him? Could he have been swaddled tight as a mummy when he was an infant and left hanging on a wall hook to urinate and defecate all because his parents were busy working, as it was in Ancient China? And is now? Disappointed in love, more likely.

Or maybe he wanted to be other than he was? She fell to her knees to get a view of his face that wasn't cast in the shadow of one of the many pines surrounding the house. Here, sitting in a faded armchair eating his breakfast, was the man she'd picked out for herself. Even if her family were here with her, not back home in Chengdu, they wouldn't be able to make this match for her.

During the half hour she watched him, he looked lost. She'd once heard him say, "The white race has had it." She'd asked him to explain "had it" and then concluded silently—it wouldn't have occurred to her so early on to contradict the professor—that all she'd seen of America so far conveyed the opposite.

Holding on to the windowsill, still stooped, she looked out toward the road; someone could be watching *her*.

Turning back, she continued to admire her teacher's long, distinguished, European sort of face. He'd eaten slowly and looked satisfied. She remembered that she had recently described his face to a friend as pale, smooth, thoughtful, sad. Her English wasn't good enough for fancy words or metaphors, and though she was tempted to show off the clichés she'd learned so far— handsome devil, cute like crazy, good catch—she knew they sounded wrong when Chinese people used them.

❖   ❖   ❖

On his lap, open and propped up by his slightly bent knees, lay a book of poetry in the original Chinese, written by a ninety- year-old Chinese woman whom Phillip was writing a book about in English. Who would read his own book was a question Phillip didn't ask; it had been made plain to him that his career teaching Chinese literature at the university depended on his being able to publish it: no tedious book, no cushy job.

He heard a knock at his door. Without spilling his breakfast, he fell to the floor. He went down dramatically, ridiculously, as though in this quiet residential neighborhood in Charlottesville, Virginia, where he rented half of a divided house, he had some- how become experienced at ducking grenades.

Only one person would come by without calling first. He knew from experience that she would eventually decide to peek through the window; this way she wouldn't be able to see him crouched next to the fireplace. He felt a bit like a bug, which, escaping one swat, fears another.

But of course she'd already seen him.

Kaidi now stood on the doorstep holding a cantaloupe. She knocked politely, patiently.

Not knowing how long she would persevere—he craved a second cup of coffee—Phillip crawled around the living room chair into the kitchen, where he could resume human posture without being seen from the front windows. Yesterday he had hidden from—avoided—one of his colleagues in the East Asian studies department by turning into the library when he'd been heading toward the bookstore. He wondered whether hiding wasn't becoming a habit with him, whether the dark moods his ex-wife had complained about were becoming darker. He put the kettle on and then, cleverly, caught it before it whistled.

There was a rap on the back door.

Phillip looked up and saw Kaidi, who had been one of the weaker students in his graduate seminar on twentieth-century Chinese literature last semester, smiling at him through the glass. He opened the door and let her in.

"I called many times on the telephone. When no answer, I grow afraid for you. I thought maybe you not love me anymore," she said in a voice that faded away shyly.

She wore a white knit top and a blue skirt. Although the skirt hit above her bony knees, it struck him as old-fashioned. Since the last time he'd seen her, she'd inserted pennies into the front flaps of her loafers. What fashion genius had told her to do that? Her straight black hair lay in strict bangs above her eyebrows and hung below her chin.

She took a knife from the drawer and split the melon in two. Baa-dooom, like an ax. Lowering her eyes, she spilled the seeds into the sink, arranged the halves on plates, and brought the fruit out to the table that took up a large corner of his living room. Kaidi dusted off her chair before sitting down.

"Sorry," he said, "I guess it's kind of dingy in here."

"You have beautiful home," she reassured him.

Phillip's sister, who'd come down from Washington to visit last week, had told him the furniture was tacky. Maybe so. He liked the large fireplace, the rows of small-paned windows across the front room. So what if the tall pines blocked out all the sunlight and mildew was a year-round problem. He liked the cathedral ceiling that he could look up at from his reading, and he liked sitting out in his own backyard (the house was built in an L shape and the landlady had the side yard). It didn't bother him that the scratched and tinny-sounding baby grand piano took up a quarter of the living room (unnecessarily, since Phillip didn't play) and that the curtains were made out of some "disgusting"—

so his sister said—fireproof material. Aside from his landlady's occasional intrusions, the place suited Phillip. He was far enough from the fraternities and sororities on Rugby Road not to be bothered by drunk undergraduates puking on his lawn, but close enough to campus to ride his bicycle. He wore a helmet. Rumor had it that female enrollment in Chinese language courses had gone up since he'd arrived.

"I don't like to talk to anyone first thing in the morning," he told her. "It reminds me of my marriage. It's a right we have in this country not to answer our doors or phones," he said, surprised to hear his own anger.

Kaidi urged Phillip to eat and then sat staring at him. Her dark eyes, surrounded by pale, sculpted flesh, looked to him like lovely animals she had no control over that happened to live inside her face. They showed signs of tears.

He heard the mail drop onto the floor in the outside hallway. When he went out his landlady had already collected it. One by one Rose handed Phillip several envelopes. After each one, she looked up at him. Phillip wasn't disposed to harsh judgment, but he knew that Rose had been examining tenants' mail and listening in on their phone calls for thirty years.

Walking back, he opened the one from his ex-wife, Cynthia Forde-Nelson. (She persisted in using his last name; they weren't officially divorced.) It was a greeting card, a happy birthday card, though May 15 was nowhere near his birthday, and his ex-wife's face, her whole upside-down body in fact, was the subject of the card. In the slick-coated photograph, his ex was lying on a wood floor wearing a pink and orange shirt with her pink-tighted legs up on a white radiator. Streams of colored ribbons curled around her. Balloons and party masks floated about the room, and the way she held the uncorked champagne bottle made the viewer think she'd been chugging from it. A man dressed similarly, with a chubby version of his ex's wacky face, had his back slouched up against the radiator. Get it? Drunk. The caption read, "It's not the years that make us older, it's all those goddamn birthday parties."

Phillip's ex was a performance artist who, because her art generated no income, did a lot of different things to make money. Posing for the funnies division of a greeting-card company was, he gathered, the latest.

Inside the card her own note read—he didn't have an answering machine, so she wrote him notes all the time now—"I hear you've got Oriental feet up and down your spine. And, that she cooks. Lucky you." One of Phillip's four sisters lived in the same building as his ex in Washington, D.C. Anne, the sister, must have told Cynthia about Kaidi.

As he saw it, Cynthia was an artist not because she produced anything of artistic worth but because her personality deserved the distinction. She didn't have a rational urge in her, and even if she had, her inclination would have been to suppress it.

It had dawned on him slowly, her almost total unwillingness to be rational. During the long year they spent together in China so that he could study, she'd insisted on communicating with the Chinese she met by mimicking them, and it was particularly frustrating to him that through all the laughter she generated (she was a terrific mimic) she'd adjusted better than he had—after all, he was the one who actually knew the language.

Her unwillingness to be rational had about driven him crazy. Mornings as he got up out of the sofa bed in their two-room apartment in the city (he'd been a graduate student during most of their marriage, and between them they barely managed to scrape together rent) it never took him long to find a sore point—her large underwire bras hanging from the pipes in the bathroom: the top drawer of her bureau was too filled with candy and snacks to hold them. If he cut his face shaving, or burned his toast, he let loose. And yet *she* called *him* repressed. Weren't temper tantrums the opposite of repression? he'd always meant to ask. He usually followed them up with a long silent period.

She herself never raised her voice or responded directly to his rage, but during his fits she sometimes sang a song she'd resurrected from her childhood. The lyrics that accompanied the up-and-down empty melody went, "Bad mood Philly-willy, bad mood Philly willy" (if his name had been Jack it would have been Jacky-wacky . . .). And she performed the song the way siblings in her own family had—by turning in a circle with her hands above her head—to urge one another out of a bad mood. The first time she'd sung it, it had worked; Phillip's smile, sliver size, encouraged her to run over and tickle him, and soon they were both laughing. After that the song made him want to strangle her.

Her unwillingness to be rational. When she learned that the Chinese used the words *mother* and *father* to swear with, she began saying, with the same emphasis other Americans give to words having to do with religion, feces, or sex, "Oh my mother," or "Oh my father." You didn't have to know Cynthia for long to realize that this wasn't a corny impulse like substituting, say, fudgsicle for fuck or signing a note with a smiling face. Mother, father—both got her juices going more than god. She made up for the fact that "mother" wasn't a bona-fide curse in English by breaking down the syllables and turning up the volume. If there was one thing everyone would agree on about Cynthia, it was that she was loud.

He still thought of Cynthia as pretty in a plain, freckly, boyish way that clashed unexpectedly with her large breasts and otherwise small body. Cynthia bought her clothes in thrift shops and dressed dramatically, whimsically, one day like a gypsy, with a purple velvet hat pinned sideways on her head, the next like a motorcycle mama in blue jeans with a tight black vest that zippered up the front. She owned a pair of lederhosen. Phillip had been drawn to her theatricality. Still, he encouraged her to wear cotton T-shirts to bed.

Her unwillingness to be rational—and then suddenly she'd say something bizarrely overrational. "If we ever had a child," she once said, "you'd have to wear a nursing vest, because if I go through nine months of bearing it, you can go through nine months of nursing it." But by then he didn't want to have a child with her. He'd already agreed to see a shrink, and in no time at all their marriage was declared hopeless.

Now she sent him notes every week or so to remind him—he assumed—of just how colorless his existence without her was. The note before this one read: "The Chinese chef at the joint I waitress at said I was a 'pillow of rafts.'" It hadn't taken him long to figure, "barrel of laughs." The message of her notes was always, "I'm having a gas. And you?"

"Bad news?" Kaidi asked.

"No, not really," Phillip answered.

"My letter this morning, bad news," she said.

"Oh," he said, not wanting to sound overly encouraging. He was becoming more and more confused about his relationship with Kaidi. For months, he'd avoided sleeping with her. On the mainland, he knew, couples restricted themselves to heavy petting in the parks at night. (Cynthia claimed that after midnight the parks in Beijing became virtual nudist colonies, but neither he nor anyone else he'd talked to agreed.) Away from home, Kaidi had been throwing herself at him. Phillip's own interpretation of the unwritten Chinese rules on premarital sex was that only actual intercourse could give her claims.

"The university grants me no scholarship for next year," Kaidi said unfolding a letter.

"Ducky . . . Ducky," he could almost hear Cynthia's voice in the background cooing at him; then the way she said Ducky (she'd almost never called him Phillip: "Ducky, Cuddle-boy, Rice Cake . . ." the list of his names went on and on) changed, and she was ordering him around. "Ducky bites donkey dung." She overused alliteration. He imagined Cynthia pretending to push a button and then go through an enactment of his body being blown to bits. "Ducky self-destructs," was what she would say about his involvement with Kaidi.

Since the beginning of the student uprising in Tiananmen Square, Kaidi had found a reason to visit him almost every day. Phillip held her hand as they compared notes on each new event. They spoke in Mandarin. She laughed at things he said. If a car in front of them didn't move as soon as a light turned green, Phillip would say loudly, "It's not going to get any greener." At home Kaidi repeated this joke and laughed again, covering her mouth, as she always did when she laughed or smiled, with her hand, her fingers spread so that he could see through them. He kissed her and wished he hadn't, kissed her and wished he hadn't.

The teaching semester was over, and though he had time to write, his book wasn't going well. He had a paper to deliver at a conference next week and hadn't started on it. And Cynthia kept finding ways of creeping back into his head. Sometimes he wanted to call her up and cry, "Help me," and at the same time he'd say, "No, leave me alone." He looked at Kaidi. He'd been looking at her all along, but now he saw her. Her elbows were red; she had a bump on her lip. With no scholarship, she'd have to return to China. Or else marry an American.

The telephone rang. He rubbed his arm muscles, sore from yesterday's workout at the gym, and answered it in the bedroom.

"You sound funny," Cynthia accused him. "Is she there?"

"Is who here?" Phillip asked, aware that his landlady had also picked up her phone and was listening.

"The woman you're seeing."

"I'm not seeing anyone," Phillip said, and then hung up on her. When he went back out into the living room Kaidi was holding the receiver of his other phone and sucking a finger.

"Yes you are," she said. "You're seeing me." She came toward him and reached her arms around his neck.

2.

Through the same window two days later she had a better view of him. She'd remembered to wipe the window clean from the inside, and now the cloud on his face wasn't dirt, but an expression. His seriousness set him apart from other Americans. If the students were successful and China did become a democracy, Phillip could go back with her and help her people recover what had been lost since the Hung dynasty. It had been wild within her, this feeling of hope. When the *Daily Progress* called her early this morning for a statement, she'd said that the People's Liberation Army would never fire on the people. There, she'd spoken out.

Kaidi brushed a cluster of pine needles from her knee and watched them fall onto the back of a brown bird. It had probably hit the window over her head and may have been lying dead at her feet on Wednesday too. She took off one of her sandals and placed the sparrow inside. She hadn't told Phillip about following hordes of older children around her neighborhood as they banged on gongs and drums to panic the sparrows. Exhausted, the birds fell to the ground, and the bigger children crushed them with their feet. Mao had ordered their destruction in his Four Pests Campaign. Rats, flies, mosquitoes—and sparrows. She would explain this to Phillip as she showed him the sparrow. He would understand the importance of such a story.

Before, when she was still his student, Phillip had tried to surprise her by pointing to various things as though she were a child: the vase in a store that looked like a paper bag, polka-dot socks, modern sculpture. True, many things in America were unusual. But in America she hadn't really been surprised by anything. Afraid, embarrassed, confused, covetous, but hardly ever delighted or surprised.

Kaidi looked away from the window when Phillip began unbuttoning his shirt. When she looked back, he was down on the floor doing push-ups. His obsession with exercise was as peculiar to her as other Americans' obsession with sex. Last week while they were watching TV, Phillip had tried to explain the difference between a transvestite and a transsexual. She knew she should have tried harder to understand, but the idea gave her a chill, like when she'd bit into her first piece of American chocolate and the foil still on it had hit a filling in her tooth. And no matter what Phillip said (about China she was always willing to contradict him), there were no homosexuals in her country.

Still, she saw she would have to change other ideas she had

about sex. Phillip never told her how she could improve herself, but she thought she knew. She looked down at her skirt—she didn't own an iron—and felt ashamed of how she looked. He was doing sit-ups now. On the outside so hard, and inside, where his soul was, soft like an organ, a heart, a muscle you could exercise only with your mind. Jumping jacks, Phillip did them in fast motion. His nipples were tiny, like a boy's. She would start at his neck and work down. He knew she'd been a masseuse before leaving China. For months he'd been teasing her about the literal translation of the Chinese word for massage: a horse killing a chicken.

❖   ❖   ❖

He was lying on his stomach, and her hands were doing large fanning maneuvers on his back. He congratulated himself for hanging up on Cynthia the other day and felt his body relax as the pressure Kaidi used grew stronger and stronger. Later, he would take notice of her hands. Even as she turned him over on the bed and began on his arms and chest, he acknowledged that massage needn't be sexual. But then, with his eyes closed, he couldn't help it, one of Cynthia's sex plays—she sometimes gave him the aggressor's role—came to his mind, and Kaidi capitalized on the result. She started undoing her own buttons. Then she raised the covers and got underneath by putting her legs together like someone getting into a sleeping bag, and she offered her small body as no woman he could imagine himself with ever would. Cynthia had always directed her own symphony. Kaidi lay still, and it was only by sheer exertion on his part that things worked at all. And then Kaidi held his hand afterward, and in his shame—he hadn't enjoyed himself—it occurred to him that he might have to marry her now.

He lived in a free country, he reasoned, wiping himself with the bed covers, who could make him marry her? He shuddered, remembering how Cynthia had been able to make him do almost anything. Phillip sat up in the shaded room. He wasn't living with Cynthia, nor, thanks to a stroke of fate, for one in four human beings was, living in China. After a year, even he found China's capital oppressive. And yet it didn't occur to him to criticize the Chinese culture the way many Westerners he knew did. He believed most Americans who'd visited China missed the subtlety and humor in the Chinese. He liked to tell his students about how, when he first went to the mainland, it was proper to blame the Gang of Four for everything that was wrong, but still improper to blame Mao. Phillip had heard many Chinese chew out the Gang of Four, but as they uttered the politically correct line, they held up the five fingers of one hand.

Phillip wanted to forget what had just taken place between himself and Kaidi, but when he pictured himself lying bare-chested on the bed, he knew that the shy way he had shown pleasure at how, for instance, she'd cracked his back by pulling at his hips—ahhh, he'd groaned—had given her encouragement. Someone like Cynthia might even consider the kind of sex he'd had with Kaidi rape. After all, her hips hadn't budged, between her legs she'd had no grip.

He got up from the bed, turned on the shower, and tried to imagine himself married to Kaidi.

"You're too gorgeous," Cynthia often told him. She used words like that—gorgeous, wonderful, fabulous. It had been painful to find out how many others she also buoyed up with her enthusiasm. It wasn't just every single one of her women friends who were won-der-ful, but also acquaintances, grandmothers, strangers . . . jerks.

He used to watch Cynthia, the mundane things she did after an afternoon of sex—tying her robe, swabbing her face with a drenched cotton pad, "yuk," and then showing him the dirt—the way Kaidi was watching him now. He knew Kaidi wouldn't barge into his shower Cynthia-style or comment on the duration of his postcoital piss. Kaidi watched him from the bed as he toweled off. He had left the door of the bathroom open on purpose so as not to shut her out. She watched him now, too, as he began to drink the glass of milk he had brought back to the bed.

The way she watched—with approval, he imagined, as he also noticed how she pulled the covers right up to her lips—made him feel good and, he hated to admit, a bit superior to her.

Cynthia put pressure on him to be more open. "How do you feel?" she said, bringing her face up so close he could smell her lipstick. "Come on, come on," she urged when he finally began to speak. But her encouragement felt like an interruption. She destroyed the possibility of intimacy between them by demanding it. There, he'd come up with an insight about her. Too late. When you ask me how I feel, I feel nothing. He took another sip and smiled, remembering Cynthia's joke about his drinking milk after sex. It replaces the semen, she teased. He wondered what it would be like to marry someone he didn't love.

"I don't think I'll ever be able to get married again," he told Kaidi. Too sudden. He hadn't wanted to hurt her. Her silence made him lean over and kiss her.

"You marry your wife and you not love her," she said.

He kissed her again because it seemed easier than an explanation.

"Chicken," Cynthia's voice rang inside his head as he drew his favorite tie up around his throat. "Wimp," she added. He bent over and pulled on the old suede cowboy boots Cynthia had given him to improve his image. (He could be a professor, but he couldn't look like one.) When he returned, Kaidi continued to stare at every movement he made. He sat down next to her on the bed and shook her arm gently. He didn't sleep with women casually. He *used* to love Cynthia. When he married her he loved her.

"I love you." Up to a certain point Cynthia had always said I love you when she went out the door, even when she went to the store to get milk—in case she got run over by a car. Over and over again, he'd said it back, proud of his new and unexpected fluency with the words. He'd never said them before Cynthia. He got so that he could say them without flinching, without thinking.

"I'll drop you off at the tennis courts," he offered. Kaidi sometimes sat for hours on the grass watching students play tennis.

"No, please," she said, "take me home."

❖   ❖   ❖

With his head inside the refrigerator, he pictured himself boiling potatoes and smothering them with butter and salt. Or he could munch on raw carrots while sitting over his computer. Phillip heard his landlady cross the hallway that separated them and knock.

"Where's your Oriental girl?" she asked, peering in.

"Her name's Kaidi."

"Peculiar girl. She stands looking in the window at you for a long time before she knocks."

It occurred to Phillip that the only way she'd know about Kaidi's habit was if she had a habit of looking out her own living room window over at him. He didn't want to prolong the conversation—he might be missing the world news. Troops were moving in on Tiananmen again, and once again the demonstrators had blocked them.

"Cynthia called," Rose said. The way she said it was like a question: Why does your ex-wife keep calling? The mention of Cynthia's name, he felt sure, had just brought on a new bout of the diarrhea he'd first gotten in China and had had on and off ever since. Would he ever get rid of it? "She said she's bringing some papers down for you to sign."

"When?" he asked. Rose didn't answer right away. He should have insisted on his own telephone line *before* taking the apartment.

"She didn't say." His landlady took out a cigarette. "I had my son put up the ladder for you." Phillip looked out the window and saw it leaning against the house. It was in the lease; he was supposed to clean the leaves out of the gutter. Phillip went back inside, smiled big for Rose, and shut the door.

Why couldn't Cynthia have put the divorce papers in the mail? Phillip called her Washington number and left a message on her machine suggesting she do that. He went into his bedroom and turned on his other TV, an old black-and-white set. He'd missed the world news but caught the local headlines. The queen of some county fair had been willing to hold the prizewinning turkey, but wouldn't make hog noises. When her big pasty face came on, Phillip decided she looked like the abducted Patty Hearst. This year's queen, a bummer on all counts.

Settled on his bed, he closed his eyes for a second. When he opened them the faces of several young black men filled the screen. Phillip doubted that crack could be so much better than drinking a couple of six-packs. When he thought of drinking, he never thought of one or two beers, but of eleven or twelve— even, given a Saturday and a doubleheader, fifteen. "Cynthia drove me to it." He tried the sentence out loud. Truth—he'd been drinking since high school. Deeper down in the half sleep, he saw himself die, not of old age or of crack, but of inertia. The idea didn't summon up any fear.

Phillip stood and blamed his dizziness on lack of food. He'd been lifting weights that afternoon. Booze control, Cynthia had called his exercise program. And he realized, feeling something close to fear, that he missed Kaidi.

He didn't want to face his work tonight. Maybe he hated writing. Maybe thinking wasn't always all that high on his list either. Several months ago he'd agreed to give a paper at a conference on children in Chinese fiction. And now he had only a few days left to figure out what he would say. The facts he'd encountered in his research kept getting in the way:

> Today (1989) millions of Chinese peasants inhabiting barren, parched lands along the lower reaches of the Yellow River are rearing babies in bags of sand.

Phillip went to the kitchen, took out his wok with the momentary fantasy of whipping up a spicy stir-fry—like one of Kaidi's with fresh ginger and Szechuan peppers. Instead he stared into the dull surface. Nothing came back.

With barely enough water for man and livestock to drink, the peasants can't spare any to wash themselves or their babies. By placing the babies in bags of fine yellow silt, which is changed daily, the peasants avoid the need for diapers. The sandbags also allow the mothers, fathers, and grandparents to till the fields for many hours each day, leaving the babies alone, safe inside their bags.

He had asked Kaidi about the sandbags. "In the north," she'd said, "the peasants are stupid."

Phillip put the wok on his head. Cynthia could make herself look like a Chinese peasant in it, stretching out her eyes and barking Chinese tones realistically—*heng,* she would say in one octave, and then an octave lower she would finish the Chinese word for "good" with a nasally *hooww.* In China, Cynthia had made many friends by imitating the language, the opera, the way they ate, with the bowl close to their mouths. Slowly, Phillip saw that she hated their opera, the way they ate; the shoveling, slurping action revolted her. Over the year being funny turned into making fun. "Racist," he wished he'd shouted at her.

Cynthia couldn't make him laugh after a while, not since the long weekend at his family's house in northern Michigan when she had managed to convince his family members that he—he of all people—was on the verge of suicide. He had gone outside before dinner to see if he could spot a wild animal—a deer or turkey—in the snow. Cynthia was inside talking to his sisters and his mother, about him—he had no doubt—tracing his moodiness to this or that event in his childhood. Then she'd somehow gotten his family all together and they had huddled in the bay window of the house to watch him as he stood still on the dock at the edge of the pond. He told himself he wouldn't return until he saw his animal, and after a few minutes when he felt his attention begin to falter he challenged himself. The Taoists believe that to remain still for a long time can bring movement, change. He tried to make himself part of the landscape. He glanced slowly down at the water, covered with a thin layer of ice. One end of his scarf swung down, swiping the snow. The rabbit he hadn't until then seen hopped into the pine forest, and Phillip heard his mother's voice calling him. Slowly, he walked toward the house. That's when he saw all of them huddled in the window.

They were overly solicitous the rest of the evening. It had taken him a while to piece things together. Cynthia cornering his sisters and telling them how he hid under the covers in the middle of the day. She would have had lots to tell them: he spits bloody phlegm; he kicks the door open when he enters instead of pushing it like everyone else; he doesn't like my art; he hates chocolate chip cookies, the only thing I know how to make. They themselves had started to recall little things—that he was pale and drinking too much. As final proof, she'd called them over to the window to witness his despair: see how close he is to the edge? See how still? What they didn't know was that watching for an animal, standing on the dock, cold on his cheeks, his big boots buried comfortably under the snow, he'd been smiling, and his penis, as if in response to the warmth that had crept up on him as he'd passed his test, had bounded slightly—just a thought—and he'd wished for more snow.

He took the wok off his head and stared into its surface again. Nothing of his own reflection came back.

> The sandbag children do not learn to sit until they are a year old,
> don't walk until they are three. Instead of talking, they scream.

"Ducky?" How could he have allowed himself to be called Ducky? Phillip put a hand to his ears. Eee-I-eee-I-owe. He repeated any old gibberish to keep her out. The hard-liner, Li Peng, had met with the student leaders to demand they end the hunger strike. Everything was a mess. The student leaders admitted they had lost control of their movement. At first, Kaidi had been hopeful about their chances—yet Kaidi herself had pointed out that her people had never understood the first thing about democracy.

The Chinese he'd known on the mainland had always given him gifts, strange, useless things—a banner with a factory painted on it—that he brought back and stored in a closet. Cynthia was like that. She gave some odd, impulsive, distorted version of love and then without saying so wanted the real stuff back. He stopped without quite finishing the idea. He'd heard a noise. Kaidi cutting the cantaloupe with the big knife. He opened all the drawers. The dishwasher, empty. He told Cynthia to be quiet, to give him time to think. He could not come up with any other explanation for it—his kitchen knife was gone.

❖   ❖   ❖

Phillip had never been to Kaidi's apartment but knew where it was. He drove quickly. Climbing the outside stairs, he brushed the railing. He drew a splinter out of his arm and pinched blood from the small wound. What would he do if he found her? Why had he made the connection: cutting the cantaloupe, the missing knife? Hoole-ly-mother. Outside lights from the apartment building next door enabled him to see the shape of the dark kitchen through the window. He went in. The drabness of the place appalled him: torn linoleum, metal cabinets with missing doors and handles, excessive tidiness and no furniture. He heard a cat meowing on the landing, and when he turned back around, he pictured Cynthia jumping athletically up onto the kitchen counter. She had a towel in her hand and was drying her face. Her short legs dangled off the edge, and she began scratching them with a certain amount of pleasure.

"Fleas," she said. "We've got fleas." It had taken them weeks to get rid of them.

The cat cried again. The flea-infested apartment he'd lived in with Cynthia was a palace compared to this. Cheerios were spilled on Kaidi's counters. Phillip ate one.

"Anyone home? Kaidi," he called, and then in Chinese, "where are you?" *Ni zai nar*, was how it sounded. *Ni zai nar*, he said again, and then silence. He walked down the short, bare hallway. Ahead there were two doors—a bathroom perhaps and her bedroom. He opened one door and walked into a closet where a single gray coat hung neatly, pathetically. He remembered Cynthia suggest-

ing that his attraction to Chinese language and culture had to do
with his liking dull things, baseball, scholarship, socialism. Gray
clothes were another example she came up with. But he knew
she meant gray personality. When he opened the second door, he
felt his heart palpitate. As his eyes adjusted to the dark, he noticed the toilet and miniature sink in one corner of the small
bedroom. There were unpatched holes in the walls. Library books
were stacked in a corner, and a piece of lace fell prettily from the
single narrow window. Phillip stepped into the room. In the
darkest corner, in a nook behind the door, was a small mattress.
Next to it a plastic lamp with a gold-fringed red shade. The three
pillows that leaned up against the wall were uncovered, and
Kaidi's clothes lay in neat piles on the other side. At first he
thought her small body was there under the covers, and then he
saw she'd left the blanket in a tangle.

"Ni zai nar." He said it again, louder to make sure. When she
didn't respond, he flicked the light switch on, and the bare bulb
overhead filled the room with terrible light. He could have been
in the bathroom of a sleazy bar. In the background, in the kitchen
perhaps, he heard a noise like the noise the knife had made when
she'd split open the cantaloupe. Ba-doom. Phillip saw his face
elongated in the cheap mirror ahead of him. The crack in it
divided him between his eyes. He went back to her bed, straightened her covers, and lay down to wait.

He felt the familiar rolling motion in his stomach—a warning,
he didn't have much time—but continued to lie in Kaidi's bed.
It was comfortable. He remembered when Cynthia had talked
him into being a part of one of her performance pieces. Several
years ago a gallery in Washington offered her her first show, and
Phillip agreed to help with it. Together they glued thousands
of mussel shells to canvases that covered the gallery wall. The
day before the performance, she told him he was one of the per-
formers.

He had allowed himself to be publicly humiliated. His body
tensed as he drifted back into the humiliated state, remembering:
Cynthia costumed in a striped bathing suit and a logo visor.

There she sat—in front of the wall of mussels—in a lifeguard's chair she'd rented from a swimming club. She instructed Phillip to sit at a plain table with his head down, like they make kids do in kindergarten for naps. On top of his head was a huge pile of sand. Cynthia had made a little house underneath the sand to protect his head so he could breathe, and he'd actually sat there for eight hours, three days in a row, like some pathetic Beckett character with a pile of sand on his head. People came into the gallery and laughed. "Who's the schmuck under the sand?" Cynthia literally looking down on him from above the whole time.

When he tried to guess what the piece was a metaphor for—relations between men and women, bourgeois leisure life—she looked at him dumbly and then groaned.

"Academics," she screamed, making big, frustrated gestures with her hands. "No wonder college-educated people are so literal-minded—they've all been taught by academics."

Phillip got up and used Kaidi's toilet. He felt much better. He looked back at the bed. It was his own impulse and not anything to do with Cynthia that led him to look under Kaidi's pillow. He'd found the knife.

He picked it up and stared at the shiny blade reflecting the harsh light. "Did it ever occur to you," Cynthia butted right in, "that your Chinese friend might go after you? Never mind carving wedges in *her* wrists. When she finds out you're not interested in marrying her, what makes you think she won't slit your throat? After all, here's the missing knife, Oh my Moth-er."

Phillip started to maneuver the knife through the air, making first slow arches like in a tai chi exercise and then hard slashing motions. He jabbed the knife forward. "You don't know what you're talking about. What about your throat?" he said louder as he again cut the air with the knife.

Maybe he heard a noise at the other end of the apartment and maybe not. He kept on, his voice much louder now. "Get"—he swung in a figure eight, taking pleasure—"the fuck out of my head."

Kaidi did make a small noise shutting the door behind her. He turned around and saw her leaning against the bedroom door, sucking a finger.

3.

Sitting on a suitcase at her place outside Phillip's living room window, she saw only the back of his television, but knew it was turned on. He lifted his hand to rub his eyes. Or was he covering them to avoid seeing? Workers, not students, had clashed with the PLA. This morning's paper said their convoys had moved into the city. She'd been wrong: the soldiers *were* preparing to attack.

Phillip didn't understand that when she said she was ashamed, she didn't mean for just herself or her family, but for her country. The three couldn't be separated. Phillip had shown so much interest in her country, she knew he felt sorry for her now. She stood and picked up her suitcase. He would let her stay.

No one from her school unit in Chengdu would have pointed to her as someone who would lead an interesting life.

No one from the beauty parlors in Beijing where she'd worked as a masseuse would have traded places with her.

No one she knew back home wanted to be thirty-three years old and unmarried.

Phillip had looked strange holding it up under the bright lights. She hadn't understood what he was saying as he swung the knife through the air. Why had he been doing his silly exercises at her house? She had not tried to explain that she had taken the knife to protect herself. Phillip always argued against her when she insisted that for speaking to the newspapers she would be punished. Already someone had followed her through campus. She wasn't brave like the other students.

When he finally saw her, he stopped moving the knife in the air. He shook his head at her as though disapproving. He thought she'd taken the knife for something bad. His eyes looked sad, and he had been—she went blank and then came up with the word—affectionate. Yes, she liked that. She liked it very much. He could think what he wanted about the knife.

She knocked on his front door.

If she ever did try to kill herself—and in America she had sometimes thought of it—she wouldn't choose a knife. There were all sorts of pills in his medicine cabinet.

❖   ❖   ❖

He answered right away.

"They're saying the soldiers want blood."

"Butchers," Phillip said in a way that made her look up at him.

Kaidi said nothing. He wished he hadn't said it quite like that, as though butchery were in *her* blood.

"I stay?" she asked, pointing to her suitcase.

Phillip looked at her severely and then broke into a teasing smile. "You stay tonight."

"I stay long time," she argued.

"We'll see," he laughed nervously.

"I stay," she told him again, landing her suitcase on the couch and zipping it open. "I bring presents," she said, shaking a half-full jar of popcorn. "American girls say popcorn makes you thin." She ducked back into her suitcase. Among her clothes, she found an article she had clipped from a recent newspaper. "It's Bing Xin," she said, pointing to a paragraph and handing it to him.

Phillip studied the picture of the old woman he was writing about. He knew things about her the students had perhaps forgotten: she'd gone to Wellesley College; her poems had inspired another movement, seventy years ago. Now student leaders had asked her to sign their statement. Over the loudspeakers in Tiananmen Square, Bing Xin's lines were being read.

After they'd slept for many hours, Phillip woke, his hand on the black hair spread out over his pillow. He got up, stood over her for several minutes, bent to touch her hair again, dressed, and left the house. The light from the street lamps seemed dimmer in the rain, and as he walked it rained harder. He heard thunder and wondered for a brief second what Kaidi would think if she woke and found him gone. She was afraid of the wind and had pointed to the two trees overgrown with kudzu that would one day surely fall on Phillip's house. He would tell her another time: by then I won't be living here. He walked on down the road. The residential area seemed unreal, like the model town he'd once built on the Ping-Pong table at his parent's home.

The lamps in the block in front of him were not lit, and he couldn't see the large stately houses on either side of the road. The road widened. He strode forward. As if with one push millions of miles into a dream. Clear to the other side; he had done something impossible. Changed his past? Then turn around! Still in the dark, he felt his way through a pedestrian walkway into the square. Though he had been here many times, the silence and the dark disoriented him. The mausoleum must be in front of him. Or was he at the far end toward Changan Boulevard. Where were the students? How would they know when the soldiers surrounded the square? Rain fell on the cement. Television footage gave no clue to how large the square was, thirty, maybe forty football fields. Now he had it, the Great Hall to the east, the student tents pitched somewhere in the middle. He heard a crackling high-tech sound through the wind. A gun being loaded? Tanks moving? Phillip looked for a place to hide. There must be a garbage site or a lavatory nearby. Then he remembered that the subway entrance joined the walkway he'd just come out of. A footstep, someone running. He couldn't see more than inches in front of him except for the black shadows flitting by, close and then far away. Frantic now to react, he lurched forward and tripped on something soft. And because the surface he hit was wet grass and not cement, he discovered what he was perhaps meant to—how much he envied the students, their cause and their grit.

He lay on the grass in the rain and tried to listen to his beating heart, but the sounds he heard came from outside himself. Hours later in a coffee shop many streets over he settled on the way he would tell it all to Kaidi.

A group of UVA students jogged past. It had stopped raining, and fog still rose from the wet streets. Cars swooshed by, and Phillip turned back down the street that led to his own.

Had he dreamed she would be there? He wasn't surprised to see her large purple car in his driveway. Moby Grape. No doubt she still called it that. Sneaking around behind it, he tiptoed over the stones and sunk into Kaidi's position outside the window.

Cynthia sat—feet up—on his couch, sipping something from a mug. Had she gotten Kaidi to make her coffee? Perched in an upright chair, Kaidi wrapped her arms around her chest as though she were cold. He couldn't hear what she said.

Eager to know, he quietly crawled around the back of his side of the house. When he got to the sliding glass door, he eased it open; the screen and the curtain hanging down one side protected him. He smelled the mildew rising off the cedar porch and sat down on its edge.

He caught the end of Cynthia's sentence. ". . . raised in a glass box."

"I don't understand," Kaidi said. Phillip didn't either.

"I don't get it myself really," Cynthia continued. "You might say it was a fashion at the time, like breast-feeding is now or like short dresses." Cynthia pointed to her own striped outfit, which looked more like a shirt than a short dress. With it she wore thick black tights and shoes like a plumber's or a janitor's. "This sort of box was in fashion for intellectuals, people who read psychology. This famous psychologist B. F. Skinner had the idea that you could keep babies in glass tanks—like aquariums. Think about it, the temperature's always right. You never have to change their diapers because they just lie there naked and pee and crap like a cat in kitty litter."

Kaidi said nothing. She leaned back, allowing her shoulders to rest lightly against the chair.

"You make fun?" she finally asked.

"Me? It's downright sane when you compare it to other things: Catholicism, for instance, or psychoanalysis. I mean it was to make care for the child—you know—easier. The air is filtered, so you didn't need to bathe the baby all that often. You never had to clean their nostrils or eyes. No beds to make, sheets to wash. America: Zip Lock bags, Pop Tarts, douches. The box cut down on stimulation. With no older sister to steal his toy away, no coffee table corner to gouge his forehead on, he was more secure, more passive too. Skinner didn't mean parents should leave the kid. You were supposed to come by and give him a hug. Naturally, the kids who were brought up in the boxes *did* get left."

"Phillip live in glass box?" Kaidi asked.

"You got it," Cynthia clapped, as though Kaidi had guessed the answer on a game show.

"Phillip tell you about sandbags?"

"Sandbags?" Cynthia asked. Phillip knew Cynthia. Kaidi must have been asleep when she arrived. Cynthia had gone through the papers on his desk and seen the article about the sandbags.

> Today millions of Chinese peasants inhabiting barren, parched lands along the lower reaches of the Yellow River are rearing babies in bags of sand.

Cynthia's mind worked like that, through associations, outrageous metaphors.

Phillip had a clear view of both women, Cynthia's exaggerated smile, Kaidi's forehead, straining. The story wasn't true. He'd grown up the son not of intellectuals but of a businessman and a housewife both of whom had been devoted to all five of their children. Phillip was used to Cynthia screwing up facts. For what? As usual, her purpose made no sense to him. Her feeling for his family (so strong she acted giddy around them) had been a crucial part of her attraction to him. With her own parents divorced and estranged, she often pretended Phillip's family was her own, introducing Phillip to strangers as a brother. She urged people to say they looked alike.

Raised in a glass box? He wondered.

"Does Phillip talk about me?" Cynthia asked. Phillip thought he'd missed something. "I think I should know what he says about me."

"I don't know," Kaidi answered.

"Did he tell you I'm funny?" she pushed.

"No," Kaidi answered, looking very worried. "I wasn't raised in a sandbag," Kaidi added, as if clarifying an earlier point.

"Box," Cynthia corrected. "I said Phillip was raised in a glass box." She drew the lines of a box in the air. "All of suburban America. It might as well have been one glass box."

Kaidi shook her head. She didn't follow.

"What I'm trying to tell you is that it's not his fault."

"What not his fault?"

Jumping up, Cynthia stepped toward Kaidi, but Kaidi refused to take her hand.

"I won't bite." Cynthia grabbed the unwilling hand and pulled Kaidi toward the couch.

"Sit," she said, patting the pillow next to her. Kaidi obeyed. "He had no real childhood, no family . . . you know, stuff." She rubbed her hands together hard to illustrate, Phillip assumed, conflict, lack of conflict. "How do you think he got this way?" Cynthia blurted out, sitting snug to Kaidi.

"He not say so," she replied. Hesitating, as though unsure Cynthia would let her go, Kaidi got up and went to Phillip's bedroom. She returned with a photograph. "He keep photograph of family near his bed."

"Men are sentimental," Cynthia responded as she studied the photograph. "That's Betsy," she told Kaidi, pointing to a tall woman. "She lives in my building in D.C. I borrow her spices. So I know. I know about all of them." Cynthia pointed to each adult. "They were all raised in boxes."

Kaidi lowered her head.

"You not good wife," she said abruptly.

Phillip thought Cynthia was going to defend herself, but she just slapped her leg with her hand and laughed.

"What an outrageous thing to say." Cynthia's mouth opened. She put her arm around Kaidi. "Let me put it another way. If he couldn't love me. . . ."

Not wanting to hear more, Phillip went around to the front

and entered the house as though he'd never heard the story his ex-wife had concocted.

Cynthia screamed in delight when she saw his face at the door, and while she smothered him with nostalgic hugs he had no inclination to return—nor did she seem to expect him to—Kaidi stood back, watching, sucking on her finger. Pulling herself together, Kaidi marched outside. Phillip understood that she would want to get away from Cynthia.

He did too. Avoiding both women, Phillip climbed the ladder his landlady had left against the house. He pulled a clump of dead leaves out of the gutter and threw it down. He cleared as far as he could reach and then climbed way up, balancing on a rung above the level of the gutter.

"I thought you were afraid of heights," Cynthia said, looking up at him from inside. She'd opened the living room window and was leaning out. In the other direction, he spotted Kaidi walking down the driveway. Strange idea, glass box.

During the climb down, staring at Cynthia's face, which kept changing as he viewed it through the rungs of the ladder, he corrected Cynthia: "*Nervous* at heights, not *afraid*." He concentrated on his balance, eager now to get to Kaidi.

"Ducky," Cynthia called from inside.

"Leave the divorce papers on my desk," he told Cynthia, and then ran to catch up with Kaidi. He had something important to ask her. She had turned the corner and was walking down the middle of the newly tarred street.

"Rice-cake," Cynthia yelled after him, her voice stretched.

He had decided to ask Kaidi if she would translate his book about Bing Xin into Mandarin. But as he began to gain on her he knew it wasn't time yet. He had a different impulse. Why not take her to town and buy her a proper present, one that cost money—new shoes, a necklace, a sundress without a back? She would look beautiful in pretty clothes.

Perhaps he already knew. The soldiers did fire on the demonstrators. That evening, American reporters would call it a massacre.

Kaidi had nowhere to go.

"Phil-lip." He heard a vague and desperate piece of Cynthia's laugh. Maybe the wind. Kaidi turned around and waited for him.

❖   ❖   ❖

That summer at his family's home in Michigan, he dove off the same dock he'd stood on while Cynthia, watching him, had determined he was suicidal, and when he broke the surface of the water, Kaidi was asking his mother (both women treaded the water comfortably) if she had ever heard of a Skinner box. His mother shook her head, spat out water, and asked Kaidi if Phillip was going to take her for a ride in a chairlift before returning to Charlottesville. When you come at Christmas, she added, Phillip will take you skiing. Kaidi laughed and shook her head at such a ridiculous prospect. She couldn't cover her smile with a hand; treading water, she needed both.

Riding up the mountain that August afternoon to see the view of Lake Michigan, Kaidi, wearing one of his T-shirts, laid down the law: no more Cynthia. Kaidi changed their phone number and wrote nasty letters in which she called Cynthia a liar. Phillip helped with the grammar.

"Can't you take a joke?" They both recognized Cynthia's handwriting on the postcard.

Generations

When Michelle Coleman's mother, Nora Coleman, was bed-ridden and dying of cancer, she paid Michelle to spy for her. Michelle was fifteen and on her way to becoming an artist like her father, but when her mother took the dollar bills from a drawer beside her bed and gave her daughter an assignment to carry out on her bicycle, Michelle put down the pad on which she had been drawing her mother in her new wig, much puffier and redder than her real hair had been, and listened to her instructions.

"Wear that," Nora said, pointing to a Russian sort of fur hat high up in her closet. "He won't recognize you." She placed a five dollar bill in the girl's hand, which—translated—meant a lot of incense Michelle would buy rather than steal from the local head shop.

Her mother would have gone over in great detail how, as a spy, Michelle should conduct herself, if she hadn't then seen her own mother's Oldsmobile pull up beside the curb. Nora took an apple from a bowl of fruit beside her bed and bit in fiercely. Then she handed it to Michelle and told her to do something with it.

"Yooo whooo," Grandmother Lee's voice sang from downstairs. Michelle put the opened fruit under the bed.

"Pray she forgot to wear her perfume today," Nora whispered to Michelle.

"Otherwise, pee yew," Michelle said, and both mother and daughter pinched their noses with their fingers.

Grandmother Lee wore small feathers in her hat that day and a cluster of birds on her large bosom that she petted in an odd

28

way—odd considering Nora's recent operation—before sitting down with Michelle on her father's bed. Michelle's parents had slept in one big bed before her mother's illness, before her hair came out in big ratty clumps that, according to her mother's instructions, Michelle spread among her father's shoes, ripping up the insoles and gluing the hairs down underneath where he would walk; that was before, too, her mother's breasts were amputated and she asked Michelle if Michelle would draw that part of her when the bandages came off. Michelle thought that her mother, who had always wanted to be a writer—she was in fact a failed writer, never having written anything—developed many peculiarities when, at age thirty-nine, she took up dying.

Grandmother Lee came to visit Nora every day and tried to warn her daughter that the more she indulged her eccentricities the further she would drive her husband away. But Michelle saw that her mother had grown angry when she was dying and that she wasn't in control; in other circumstances, Nora would not have allowed herself to fight with Lee. Like the cancer, Lee had finally gotten under Nora's skin.

That day when Lee sat down next to Michelle on the bed and gave her a kiss, Michelle didn't wipe it off her face with the back of her hand. She let it stay stuck to her cheek, an orange mark to go with Lee's shoes. Michelle flashed on other kisses: open-mouthed kisses that took place, though less and less often now, in the Colemans' basement with the boy who, when they were really kids, used to dress up in Michelle's pink tutu. Michelle considered her grandmother handsome and supposed that in her own bossy way Lee was also wise. But for Nora to die so long before her own mother, that wasn't right, and so she sided with her mother against Lee.

"Well," Lee said, standing, "I came to get your blue dress."

"My blue dress," Nora said in her deadest voice, full of suspicion.

"My cousin Lisa should have it. She has so few clothes and it would look just right on her. Those eyes."

"It's Mom's dress," Michelle said. It terrified her, her grandmother's willingness to cause trouble. Lee had already opened up Nora's closet door and, having found the sparkling blue dress full of swing and style, held it up against her own much too big body. Nora, her arm attached to an IV and too weak anyway to move from her bed, looked to Michelle.

"I'll leave it to Lisa in my will," Nora said, seeing that her only child was powerless.

"Don't be silly," Lee said. "Don't be so selfish. Your own vanity brought this upon you, and now you should repent. Generosity," Lee dictated, wiping her stony eye as she stuffed the blue dress into her big purse bag; unwrapped candies, Michelle knew, stuck to its leather bottom.

Now, after many months of visiting every day, Lee had finally said it. Michelle knew it had been there, hanging in the air—the unsaid thing—slowly driving Nora mad, and now it had been said. Lee was saying that Nora had brought death upon herself.

When Lee left, Nora closed her eyes. To Michelle she looked altogether different with her eyes closed; death seemed a possibility then, as it did not when they were open, flashing with feeling—anger, mostly, and some love, Michelle let herself think. But then they opened and Michelle waited for instructions.

"When I was your age," her mother said, "my mother would flap her big hands up and down my body saying, as though it were my doing, 'You've no chest child: you are as flat as a board.'" Michelle saw her mother shudder from the memory of those hands upon her.

"Don't bother about her," Michelle said, petting the hairs backward on her mother's arm. Michelle thought her mother's little nose was so sweet, her skin so white and smooth.

"You're in style with that hair," Michelle told her. "Last year hair was either white or black, now it's red."

"You think it suits a dead lady?"

"Not dead, dying," Michelle corrected. "Don't you want me to go spy on Dad?"

"Not today," Nora said. "Take your bicycle to Mother's and get my dress back. I want my blue dress."

As Michelle turned to go, Nora pulled her gently back and

unwrapped the scarf Michelle wore around her neck. The older woman smiled at the vast hickey the scarf hid and then said, "Not little Graham?" Michelle nodded.

"You'll do better."

"You sound like Granny," Michelle said, thinking that this scrutiny wasn't so much different than hands thumping over her mother's own young body.

On her way to her grandmother's she rode by Graham's house and saw his younger brother throwing a rubber ball up against the brick. She waved, thinking they'd never done anything much in his house, only hers: on the pile of old clothes in the vast basement, which was painted—floors, walls, and ceilings—a deep nightmarish red. Clara, the Colemans' housekeeper, made Michelle eat dinner on those nights when her parents were still going out to parties together. Afterward, Michelle stuck her finger down her throat, for she knew Graham had crawled through the basement window and had the incense and candles lit. She wanted her stomach to be completely flat when his hand—so slowly she thought he would never reach—made its way down.

Michelle pushed her bike inside the bushes lining one side of her grandmother's front lawn. Without checking the garage for Lee's car, she decided that whether Lee was home or not there would be a way to get the dress. So she snuck in the basement door, up the steep, carpeted stairs that led to the old black rotary phone in the hall. To the right lay Lee's kitchen, her kingdom, Michelle thought. Michelle stopped there to listen. Hearing nothing, she went on. She ran past the grand piano at one end of the living room where Lee often sat playing thunderous music in her sloppy way, on up the stairs, and quietly down the long, wide hall that led to the master bedroom. Now she heard water running through the pipes of the old house. And suddenly she heard a man's voice. It was alive, Michelle decided, not radio or television.

Michelle slid into the room on her right, where her mother had slept as a child and where Michelle, also as a child, had spent many hours playing games with her dark-haired cousin. Her cousin used to make Michelle scream as often as she could get away with it, standing on Michelle's hands in sturdy red oxford shoes.

And so Michelle thought at first that it was her own screams she heard. The screams filled the room as she walked over to a small picture of her mother, standing with arms at her sides, wearing a uniform skirt and white blouse, more beautiful, Michelle thought, than she herself would ever be, even though her mother's mouth was open: screaming. Michelle took the picture off the wall to stop the noise. Now it was hers to keep.

She stood at the doorway listening to her grandmother's confident voice resound, full of different accents from her travels around the world, and crept slowly toward it. She peeked into Lee's room and saw nothing. Again, a man's voice. They were in the dressing room. The bathroom door was open, and water gushed voluminously, so that she couldn't make out what they were saying.

Lee's bedroom was filled with smells. "She doesn't wear deodorant," Nora once told Michelle, "and she won't take her clothes to the cleaners. She's too cheap." But that smell, so strong, was hers alone: from the little particles of face powder, from the perfume mixed with body odor and smoke from the little brown cigars she puffed on during bridge games. Unlike her mother, Michelle didn't mind the smell. It went with the antiques and the old stained carpets and the sense she had that secrets were still hidden here by her grandmother, who would not, if she could help it, allow anyone else to keep secrets. For instance, Michelle thought, Lee had given Nora away.

"Your father would have loved her anyway," Lee told Michelle the morning her mother came home from the hospital with her chest wrapped in bandages. Michelle had stayed the night with Lee, and Lee had insisted on making porridge that morning.

"I don't like it," Michelle said.

"Of course you do," Lee answered with a little laugh, pushing the brown sugar at her granddaughter with a smile. Michelle made no effort to eat it and went and made herself toast.

"Clara told me you were stubborn about food," Lee said, having taken over the porridge herself.

"What do you mean, Dad would have loved her anyway?" Michelle asked.

"Oh, well, she was so accomplished, after all. Singing, painting, athletics. And then she got the idea of writing. She never wrote a word. Certainly, he would have loved her without the operation."

"But there was no choice, the cancer," Michelle explained.

"I mean the first operation, between marriages. It was before you were born."

Michelle took a bite of toast, knowing Lee had told her something she wasn't supposed to tell.

Michelle walked carefully across the room looking for the dress. Once in the middle, she was caught by fear. She leapt to the far end and struggled to open the door to the balcony. It looked out into the park where she'd learned as a child to skate, all of them, even Lee and Nora, wearing hockey skates and carrying sticks. Outside now, Michelle knelt down in front of the gauzy curtain that covered the glass door and looked in as though watching television. From this spot, she saw where her grandmother had thrown down the big black purse with the blue dress still stuffed inside. A minute later, Lee herself walked in, in her slip, and began to undress. Before ducking, Michelle saw Lee's rounded and rolling stomach and mountainous breasts, the translucent skin all lined with blue, as though you could almost see the blood running through her, pumping her full of strength, and then her thin legs; voluptuous, she must have been. Lee put on a robe and disappeared again. She'd turned the bathwater off, so Michelle thought it was safe to sneak in. Opening the door a crack, she reentered the room, lit up now, its smell much stronger than before. She went straight for the dress. Her hand was on it when a man came out of the dressing room.

"Excuse me," he said, walking past her, then up the stairs to the third floor.

Michelle actually saw the bathroom door open and would still have had time to run before Lee stuck her head out, but the strange man had confused her. Seeing Michelle, Lee came out fully—she had no sense of modesty—and with a laugh, both friendly and imposed upon, wanted to know what Michelle thought she was doing.

"You shouldn't have taken it from her," Michelle said.

"Oh, well then, if you think I shouldn't have, tell me why."

"The dress was just an excuse. You wanted to blame her out loud," Michelle said.

"For killing herself? Yes, I guess I did."

"If she could choose to live, don't you think she would?" Michelle asked.

"She can't though now, can she?" With that Lee walked into the bathroom, meaning Michelle to follow, and plunked herself down into the water. With her white hair piled high and the weight of her big body raising the water so that it splashed out onto the floor, she leaned back and sighed with pleasure, her breasts like buoys fallen on their sides. Although Michelle sided with her mother in all things now, something about her grandmother—a warmth and elegance equal to a rich man's power—made her get down on her knees and wipe up the spilled water with the bath mat.

"I'm so proud of you," Lee said cheerfully. The ponytail sticking straight up from the top of Michelle's head was level with Lee's own bun. "It's cute," she said, petting the tuft on top of Michelle's head. "Of course I don't pretend to understand today's styles. So much blond is wearisome. Did I tell you how proud I am of you? For your art prize. A whole year of school in Switzerland."

"I'm not going, Granny."

"You'll see when it's all over. You wait and see." Lee shifted in the bath, and more water spilled.

"I saw a man," Michelle said, gesturing outward.

"Pierre Lavalle. Quite a scream really. My first boarder. He's French Canadian and a poet. Would you like to meet him?" Lee sat up amid great waves, stood, and toweled off still standing in the dirty bathwater.

Michelle shook her head, but by the time Lee was dressed and had finished making tea, spreading all kinds of cookies on a tray, Pierre had joined them. He sat, his legs straddling the piano bench, his big black cowboy boots out of place in Lee's living room, Michelle thought, when Lee handed him a cup of tea. Behind Lee's back he quickly crossed his legs, stuck his pinkie out from the delicately flowered china, and pursed his lips. Michelle smiled.

"I was sorry to hear about your mother," he told Michelle politely.

"You should have seen her mother when she was Michelle's age," Lee said. "We couldn't get her out of that tree." Lee pointed to a large oak tree whose secondary branches swooped gracefully toward the house. "All the neighborhood boys were in love with her. It was as though when they saw her monkeying up the tree like that, they saw themselves and couldn't resist.

"Nora married a man before she finished college, and he took her to Australia. She came back without him. First thing, she went and had the operation. I suppose it was done tastefully enough. She didn't tell me she'd had it done of course. I took her shopping for clothes one day to find out for sure. I had to spend hundreds on her to get her to let me into the dressing room. Later that year, she married your father. He wasn't famous then. If she couldn't be an artist herself, she could at least marry one." Neither Pierre nor Michelle said anything. "If she couldn't be an artist," Lee continued even more aggressively, "she'd at least be a work of art." She sucked at her tea loudly.

"She doesn't want to lose her," Pierre explained to Michelle. Michelle kept on eating cookies.

"He'll make a fortune off her death, painting all those diseases on the canvas," Lee said.

"You didn't have to bring Dad up," Michelle suddenly objected. "No one asked about him."

"Pierre knows everything, Michelle. Who do you think I've turned to through all this."

Michelle was used to being polite to some of her father's painter friends, so although she found Pierre both ugly and strange, she didn't mind the attention he paid her over tea. She liked his laugh. He made a joke about a politician Michelle had barely heard of and then laughed harder than either Michelle or Lee. She could see when he opened his mouth that his teeth were bad, or at least very crooked. She put him in the much-too-old-for-her category. But then Lee casually mentioned that he'd already had a book of poems published. Lee obviously thought this was impressive for someone his age. Michelle asked him how old he was and then considered twenty-four in a way she never had.

When they'd finished all the cookies, Pierre offered to drive Michelle home. Michelle agreed without mentioning that her bicycle was stuffed inside the hedge. Alone with him in his beat-up car, Michelle wished she hadn't accepted. He didn't say anything to her, not a word. She looked at the rubber dinosaurs, spiders, birds, and grotesque space creatures he had glued all along the dashboard. Reaching out to touch one, she turned to him.

"I'm a fetishist," he said, shrugging.

It was mean of him, she thought, using a word she didn't know the exact meaning of. During that short ride, she became very afraid of him.

❖   ❖   ❖

The next day, Michelle waited until Clara had changed her mother's sheets and helped her into one of the many new gift nightgowns. With great ceremony she danced into her mother's room, placing the blue dress as though it were a sacrificial offering on the end of the bed.

"Put it on," her mother laughed. "Go on, put it on for me." Michelle did as she was told, and turned around for her mother to zip it up. She stepped back and twirled. The skirt rose and followed her movement in a lovely arch.

"Let me see you," her mother said, moving her head awkwardly. "You fill it out," she said. "You fill it out all on your own," she said, smiling.

"What I went through to get it," Michelle said in a self-dramatizing voice. "And she caught me red-handed. I felt like such an idiot."

"That's her forte," Nora said.

"Pierre says she says mean things because she can't stand to lose you."

"Pierre?" Nora asked.

"Lee's taken a boarder. Pierre Lavalle, a poet."

"Is he young?"

"No. He's twenty-four," Michelle answered.

"That's young, Michelle. Do you like him?"

"Mother," Michelle objected.

"I mean, do you think of him?"

"He scares me. He's like a hoodlum, long hair, sort of sticking out on top, and black boots. He looks at me as though he knows me, and he talks to Lee about everything. I heard them when I went to get the dress yesterday." Michelle bent over to smell the new lilies on Nora's bedside table.

"Was Dad here yesterday?" she asked, realizing that this was what the lilies meant. Nora looked away.

"What did he want?" Michelle demanded to know.

"He seemed to want to convince me that he was painting like a fiend."

"Did you ask him about Blaise?" Michelle asked.

"Yes. 'Since when did you imagine I'd taken up with a man?' was what he asked me. Michelle, you didn't tell me Blaise was a man."

"I couldn't really tell. The windows were a bit dirty. Dad put his arm around her—him, I mean. They ate lunch together another time. And I told you about when I saw them laughing so hard at the back of the studio that she fell off the chair."

"He," Nora corrected again.

"So Dad isn't having an affair?"

"'Him? Her?' I told him, 'I don't know you at all anymore.' That's what I told him Michelle. He cried a little bit and then he took off his shoe."

"No!" Michelle laughed.

"'Your hair,' he said. 'I keep finding your hair in my shoes. Did Michelle do this?' he wanted to know. He was pulling little clumps out. 'All sixteen pairs,' I told him, proudly. 'Oh Nora,' he said, as though he suddenly felt sorry for me. And he put his hand on my chest. He always used to touch me, Michelle, not just there, everywhere, and hold me. We were very physical with one another, your father and I. But I told him, ever since the operation, I told him not to touch me. So last night, when he put his hand, well, I couldn't stop myself. I started screaming. He put his hands all over me then. I didn't know what he was doing and I kept on screaming."

"I heard you Mother. All the way at Granny's I heard you," Michelle said, thinking of the little picture of her mother she'd pinched off the wall. Already she'd set it up beside her bed, knowing that with her mouth wide open like that Nora was less a work of art than the woman Michelle would always fear becoming.

"Michelle," Nora said, "Could you do something for me?"

"I can't go spy on Dad anymore." Michelle ducked down below the top of the bed so that her mother couldn't really see her and crawled around to the other side. "See," she said, suddenly popping upright at the end of the bed. "I didn't fool you at all and you're bedridden. Everybody always knows what I'm up to." Michelle looked at the ten-dollar bill her mother held in her hand. Nora laughed and shook her head, but before she could explain what she wanted, she began coughing.

"Clams," she said, after spitting into the metal bowl beside her bed. "That's what your father called them. He was always spitting up clams. It was the only thing about him I found disgusting, till now. Now, I find everything about him disgusting."

"You don't," Michelle said. "Remember the picnic in South Carolina on the beach. You and Dad had drunk all that wine. You kept toasting him because he'd just sold the backyard paintings. He poured sand over your legs so they wouldn't burn up. You two were laughing. He kept roaring out that he was a sea monster. We teased him because he couldn't even swim. Some sea monster."

"Do it, Michelle. Oh, do it for me. The curtain will be the sea. You can put on my old bathing suit. And here," she said, throwing one of her pillows onto the floor. "The pillow will be your father."

"OK," Michelle said, "but, I don't want to be paid."

"I'll put it in the drawer for you." Nora said. "Whenever you need it."

Michelle walked into her parent's large closet and found her mother's many bathing suits. She put on a plain black one, took a blanket from the chest at the back of the dressing room closet, and spread the blanket down on the big rug. Michelle took the pillow, her father, and threw it toward the curtains, the sea. She heard her mother gasp, but continued the play.

"He can't swim," the woman in the bathing suit yelled to the imaginary little girl. "The crazy man knows he can't swim," Michelle screamed in her mother's voice. Standing on the blanket, which was the beach, she ran along the edge and then plunged herself into the cold water. A minute later, appearing out from behind the curtains with the pillow in her arms, she moved slowly as though dragging a large weight through the waves. Michelle brought the body onto the shore and held it tight.

Nora clapped. "You did it beautifully," she said.

Michelle put on her mother's bathrobe and picked up the blanket and the pillow. "Don't you see what it means. He trusted you to save him. It was a game and he trusted you that much."

"He was drunk," her mother said. It was obvious to Michelle that she had cheered her mother up.

"Do another one," Nora asked.

Instantly, Michelle pulled the writing desk from its place up against the wall. She put chairs on either side of it and the vase of lilies in the center. Then she changed into one of her mother's casual summer dresses and high-heeled shoes. She put one of her father's sports jackets over the other chair and balanced a beret on top.

"We're having dinner. Your father and I," Nora guessed, watching Michelle pretend to pour, swirl, and then sip the wine.

"Yes, and your seven-year-old girl has just padded in to say goodnight," Michelle filled in.

"He wouldn't wear the hat then, if we're in the house," Nora said. Michelle knocked the hat off the chair.

"Goodnight Chell," Michelle said in imitation of her mother's voice. "I'll read you the story in the morning before school." Both Michelle and her mother laughed.

"I never could get through a whole story, could I?" Nora admitted.

"The point is, Mom, that no one gets stories read to them before school instead of before bed."

"Your father and I used to go out so much," Nora explained.

"I loved watching you come down the stairs, all dressed up. I tried to entertain Dad while he was waiting for you to get dressed so that he wouldn't get mad at you for taking so long," Michelle said, putting the table and chairs back where they belonged.

"Do Baba," Nora demanded suddenly.

Michelle wound a scarf around her head turban style to hide her ponytail and then, rummaging into her mother's makeup bag, found lipstick. She touched it firmly to the center of her forehead, leaving a deep red mark. Then she sat herself down and with a certain amount of difficulty got into the lotus position. Michelle's face remained still and serious throughout. She tried to be a statue.

Nora was laughing. "I wish you'd met her, Michelle. I should have taken you with me to India."

"Lee says she was a fake," Michelle said, untangling her legs.

"There she goes again," Nora said.

"Actually, that's not exactly what she said. She said you could have gotten everything you needed from the Protestant Church if you'd wanted to, but that you had to be different."

"You'll see, Michelle. You'll see for yourself that she's wrong. All she cares about now anyway is food. Do Lee eating for me Michelle. Oh, do her eating."

Michelle laughed as she brought to mind the image of Lee at work on her dinner. But Michelle had also been thinking that they would need more clothes and props for this game if they were to do it right. So she ran down to the basement and gathered costumes and background materials. But by the time she brought them back a whole vanful of people from the hospital had arrived and they were wheeling in equipment. It was time to hook her mother up to the morphine pump. "She's lost more weight," a nurse Michelle recognized took time to explain.

In the midst of the commotion, Michelle went out into the hall. She heard whistling downstairs. Hadn't her father sometimes whistled? From the top of the landing, she recognized not her father, but Pierre. He told her that Lee had asked him to come over and take her to a three-dimensional film playing at Ontario Place. It was just like her. In the car, Pierre explained that Lee thought it would be good for her to get out of the house. However, he had no intention of sitting through such a movie. So she went with him while he drove thirty miles north of the city to the home of a friend. There he'd arranged to trade his car for his friend's motorcycle. Michelle rode home on the back, hugging him from behind, wondering what he would do if it rained.

❖   ❖   ❖

"'On my summer vacation,'" her mother said as Michelle entered the room carrying yet another box of clothes, "'I watched my mother die.'"

"They don't have you do that in grade 12," Michelle said flatly. "Now," she continued, as though unbothered, "what one do we do next?"

"Do when I first met your father," Nora suggested.

"But I wasn't there."

"I'll narrate. I was sitting in a café on Young Street trying to write down all the things that happened to me in Australia."

As her mother talked, Michelle changed her shoes, put a big colorful scarf around her neck, pulled a baggy wool sweater over her head, and sat her mother down in a casual thoughtful pose, pen in hand, occasionally sipping from a pretend cup of coffee.

"Suddenly," Nora continued, "a man who looked like an art student—not everyone in those days looked like an art student—ran over to my table and grabbed the pencil from my hand. 'Tell it to me instead,' he said, and dragged his chair closer to me."

"Is that when you pulled the chord on the streetcar?"

"On the way home, he tried to kiss me and there was no one else in the car."

"Let's say that, from now on, I have to have been there for it to count." Nora agreed with the new rule, and they both fell silent for a minute trying to think up a situation or character. Clara came to the door to say a man was calling for Michelle.

"Graham?" Nora asked.

"No," Clara said eagerly. "Some punk guy with," she paused and made flicking motions with her hands above her head, "hair, a lot of hair."

Michelle went down to meet Pierre, and he held out his hand for her to shake as her parents' friends sometimes did.

"Lee told me you asked a lot of questions about me. Lee doesn't know what I've done and haven't done," Michelle told him abruptly.

"I like every one of your earrings," he said, ignoring her comment, putting a finger on the row of earrings that curved around the rim of one of Michelle's small ears.

"You like them the way I liked the zoo you used to have on your dashboard. What do you think your friend will do with the animals?" Michelle asked.

"Outgrow them," he laughed.

"My mother warned me you might come. She said she gathered from what Lee said about you that you were *very* ambitious. She said if you were interested in me it was only because of who my father is."

"What do you think?"

"My mother also says that any older man who's interested in a fifteen year old can't get ones his own age."

"Your mother doesn't think much of you, does she?"

"Wrong," Michelle told him.

"Come on," he said, "I want to show you something."

"Don't you have a job?" Michelle asked.

"Someday," Pierre told her with a bit of impatience, she thought, "you'll marry a stockbroker."

"What's that supposed to mean?" Michelle asked.

"The daughter of an artist, what better way to rebel? And you'll look back on me. . . ." The sound of his motorcycle drowned him out, and Michelle chose to leave her supposed fate a mystery. She waved up to her mother, who had somehow managed to lift her head up to watch her daughter from the window. Michelle got on behind Pierre without knowing exactly how she'd encouraged him or how he'd convinced her. But there she was, going along, wanting to see what would happen.

Afterward, Michelle was a little ashamed of how easy it had been for Pierre to seduce her. But, she told herself, when you're that afraid of someone, it's easy for him. And he'd whispered things to her. Like how he knew how to make a woman happy. She didn't like being called a woman. Her mother and grandmother were women. Anyway, she'd been curious. Her own fears aroused her and she went with him up to her grandmother's attic and made love with him alongside his stacks of books. He had hundreds of books piled neatly over her grandmother's cast-off furniture. They hadn't been able to stop the bed from making noises, and at first this made her laugh.

"You have," he paused, "such breasts."

"What are they like?" she asked him. He didn't answer immediately. "Isn't everything like something if you're a poet?" she asked.

"Marmoreal mounts," he said. "And the tips: love's blossoms."

"What if they weren't real. If you knew I'd had an operation to make them this size and shape."

"The tonsils of a giant," he continued, lowering his voice and opening and closing his fist to make the image of the giant's mouth more tangible.

"I'm serious," Michelle said, slapping at his roaring hand. "What if they weren't real?"

"Then I'd think you were silly," he told her.

"And vain?"

"Yes, and vain."

"When you have that done, it's hard to detect cancer," Michelle told him. Pierre put his finger over her mouth.

"Lee already told me," he said, but Michelle could tell it embarrassed him to talk about what her mother had done. His own metaphors hadn't embarrassed him. She looked at him again and found beauty in his face, the black eyebrows growing almost without interruption straight across his brow, the long thin nose, and the heaviness of his chest.

"Did you put that up there," she asked him, pointing to a chin-up bar squeezed into the doorway.

"Yes. You didn't think your grandmother had, did you?" he said, looking at her. She felt proud of the way he looked at everything so closely. Then he ruined it. She saw him struggle for pleasure so many times that eventually, in the midst of her own discomfort, she started to think of her dying mother. He dropped them beside the bed, all the wet rubbers. She was glad he'd taken care of that himself. Safes, safe sex. It had been drummed into her. She couldn't stop herself from peering down at them. Her mother's clams. Her mother screaming. She let Pierre catch his breath and then slid out from underneath him. She was angry as she put her legs into her blue jeans, the knees showing through large holes. She tucked her T-shirt in. Pierre held up her bra, dangling it from his fingers, laughing, trying to coax her back. She'd already gone.

Michelle rode home on her bicycle, standing up so that the seat wouldn't hit her where it burned. Good thing her friends were away and would never know about Pierre. Even if Susan had been in the city that summer, she didn't think she would have had her over. Michelle had told Graham there was a red X on their front door. Cancer isn't contagious was what he'd said back. The red X meant death, didn't he know?

At the top of the stairs Michelle smelled flowers and saw that the door to her mother's room was closed. As cheap as Lee was, she often brought Nora beautiful roses, so Michelle knew by the smell that Lee was in with her mother. Michelle wanted to shower before going in, and yet, her mother might need her. She stood outside the door.

"What will you do when she goes to Switzerland?" Michelle heard Lee ask Nora. Michelle's year-long trip, planned for the first week in September, was something Michelle and Nora had avoided talking about.

"I'll be gone by then," she answered quietly, and Michelle thought of the device that was keeping her mother alive.

"Don't be silly," Lee said. "Your cheeks are full of color today. Have you seen that young friend of Michelle's around lately. Have you even heard her speak of him?"

"No, come to think of it, I haven't," Nora said. "I dreamed she rode off on the back of a tarantula." Michelle stifled a little laugh.

"I think she's given Graham the heave-ho," Lee remarked.

"That was bound to happen."

"Don't you see that you're making her strange. Cooped up in here for hours with you every day playing dress-up. It's not good for the child."

"She's not a child," Nora said.

"Enough of this nonsense," Lee said. "All your life you've done things to get people's attention. When I think of all those years you practiced yoga and meditation, pretending to be married to religion instead of him. It's not that easy."

"It's one way to cope," Nora argued, her voice weak.

"And now you push him away and pay her money to do things for you." Lee raised her voice over the word *money*. Michelle heard her mother sigh. Both Michelle and Nora knew the money was just extra, something her mother could give because she felt she had little else. And now Lee made it sound criminal.

"You've tried hard to keep up this image of a woman, like something a man takes with him to war. You should want some part of us to die with you."

"You don't think it will?" Nora asked, her voice so weak Michelle wasn't sure she'd heard.

"You've always created little dramas to give meaning to life. But they take meaning away. They make people angry afterward."

"You're thinking of the time I went to the ashram?" Nora asked.

"It was so sudden."

"It wasn't sudden. I'd been thinking about it for a long time."

Michelle remembered well. Her mother had packed her bags one day about three years before and disappeared for six months. Of course they knew she was in India. Michelle wrote letters. Clara was hired to run the house.

Michelle heard hard breathing from inside the room. And then a flurry of activity as though her grandmother were kicking things around. Yes, that was it. Her grandmother was kicking the boxes of clothes Michelle had dug up for their scenes. She rummaged through them, throwing costumes aside. Was she looking for something? Michelle heard the sound of ripping. She supposed Lee began with the blue dress.

"It's the money, isn't it, mother?" Nora said, straining her voice.

"It is and it isn't," Lee answered, kicking at the boxes as she reached in to tear the clothes. "I might have resented him leaving you all his money once. But we were divorced, and so I expected that, when he died, it would go to you. But now you're going to do it to Michelle. You'd never have become this, don't you see, if you hadn't had all that money. And to just give it to her with no age stipulation, no rules of use, is, frankly, well, it will ruin her."

"I want her to be free."

"Pouf, free," Lee said with great violence. "These are nothing." Again Michelle heard the sound of tearing. "Nothing," she screamed, again picking up the clothes and tearing.

Michelle still had her hand on the doorknob when the unfamiliar sound of Lee's great sobs became audible.

"Nora," Lee whispered.

Michelle didn't need to look in. Her mother had died to the sound of Lee tearing up clothes. She should go in now and comfort Lee. Lee should comfort her.

Instead, Michelle went to take a shower. It's what she'd been meaning to do all along. She took off her sandals, pants, shirt and stepped into water so hot her delicate skin went pink. She slid soap over her body and then stood still, her face tilted up into the stream. Behind somewhere, she heard the heavy sound of Lee clomping through the house. And then Michelle heard the tearing noise, like a small terrible scream inside her head. When she finally turned the water off, she heard fists banging at the bathroom door. They were calling her. Lee's and her father's voices calling her.

"Go away," she cried out, lengthening the final sound until she became aware of her mouth. Facing the mirror, she wrapped a towel over her head, another around her body, and waited. When she opened the bathroom door and stepped out of the steam she found to her surprise that she'd achieved a moment of silence. No water, no tearing, no screaming.

Kneeling on Rice

Early the day their mother-in-law planned to visit, the two women performed a rain dance in bikinis on the porch. Catherine's wide athletic movements didn't match Judy's rhythm-beating steps. In minutes they were out of breath and leaning on one another. The porch faced the bay, and none of their neighbors living on nearby farms could have seen them twisting to Bob Marley and the Wailers. It was August. Around the southern portion of Georgian Bay, Ontario, a heat wave had set in; it had been Judy's idea to go out early and invent a rain dance. When Catherine had pointed to the bright sails of windsurfers a mile or so downshore, her face had looked alarmed, as though she'd spotted the fins of sharks. Normally neither of them paid much attention to the seasonal tourists who used the rooftops of their cars to transport skis in the winter or windsurfers in the summer. Judy and Catherine lived here all year round. They were concerned now about their mother-in-law's visit. She hadn't mentioned in her letter what time she would arrive.

At noon, they looked out the window and wondered if the brief drumming—a couple of splashes—was a result of their rain dance. Judy, who was at least ten years younger, tall, thin, with dark hair and eyebrows, and even, pale skin, turned to stare at Catherine, whose big freckled arms were blotched by the heat. Judy knew that this musical burst of rain was nowhere near enough to save the corn that grew everywhere in the fields below the Blue Mountains.

Catherine let out one of her frequent deep sighs while she listened for the sound of their mother-in-law's car. Judy and Catherine had been married, at different times, to the same man.

The cats, which had belonged to Jonathan, the husband first of Catherine and then of Judy, humped on the braided rug underneath the large wooden dining table. Jonathan had married Catherine and then, after a divorce, Judy, who was, at the time, an art student in Toronto. Their husband had died in a tragic accident the winter before last. It was Judy's belief that the cats used the thick legs of the table to form imaginary lines over which the other must not cross.

"A childhood game. Two words."

"Red Rover," Judy answered.

Catherine mentioned, as they sat down together and tried to fill in the crossword puzzle, that the cats meant to kill one another. Through the huge screened windows plugged with rain the two women watched the bay. The sun swept out, breaking a cloud in two. Judy asked Catherine to remember how their husband thought the sound of waves had cooled him off like a fan. When Judy got up and ran water to make lemonade, she thought of the corn kernels, toothlike, puckering in the fields behind the brick farmhouse, and like many things the thought of the blight made her cry. She resolved as she stirred fiercely not to let Catherine see.

"Hop scotch," Judy said, turning around with three glasses hitting on a tray. She put the tray down on the crossword puzzle.

"Sweetie, qu'est-ce que tu as?" Catherine asked.

"The thought of his mother spoiling everything," Judy answered. She took a handful of cookies and dumped them on a plate.

"Do you think she'll want the house? Where will we go?" Catherine asked, twirling a piece of her gold hair around her finger tightly so that like a rubber band it stopped the blood.

"Will we stay together?"

"You keep asking that," Catherine answered, raising her voice.

"Because I want to know," Judy replied. She stood with her feet set together.

"I want to know if we're going to have the child," Catherine shouted. Judy covered her ears. Catherine then shuffled in large blue fluffy slippers, once chewed by her dog, into a small den full of books—Jonathan's old study off the dining room.

Alone, Catherine began stuffing envelopes and licking them as fast as a machine, as though she were still head of fund-raising for Canadian Public Radio. Now she just handled mailings for nonprofit groups. Recently, though, she had decided to take in boarders. Judy hated the idea. Hardly a day had gone by since her husband's death when Judy hadn't had to remind Catherine that she, Judy, was an artist.

❖   ❖   ❖

Wearing a hat to shade her head, Judy left the house to pick berries for the guest she dreaded. For all Judy knew, Catherine was still in the study licking stamps. As she walked toward the rows of raspberry bushes, Judy thought the sun cruel—it flattened surfaces, making the landscape unsubtle and without shadow, like television. The sun penetrated her. It was killing the corn. Before she even began picking, she longed for the shade. The lightness of her skin—the color of bone—was exaggerated by the red lipstick she wore and by the charcoal pencil lines drawn under and over her eyes. Witchy, he had called her fondly, making her feel exotic while she was to him, all that time, warm and accessible. She didn't belong here. It sometimes seemed to her that she got poison ivy without going outside, and she swore the cankers inside her mouth were from being near the cows. But she loved it here: home.

As Judy started to pick berries, she wondered why they had all addressed him by different names. She had called him Jack, while Catherine called him Ed, and his mother—who might at any moment be turning into the driveway—called him at all times by his full name, Jonathan Edwards.

Dr. Edwards, as Judy explained to new people in town, had been killed in a skating accident the winter before. Hearing Catherine warn him about the temperature, Judy had then watched her husband skate out onto the bay. With the hockey stick he carried, he slapped a puck back and forth; from the house, she'd seen only the back of his ballooning pants, so far, so eagerly, had he been bent forward. Tapping the puck out further than he perhaps meant to, he had stretched his stick onto thinner ice. He fell forward into the water as the ice broke in holes beneath him. There had been no sound until Judy and Catherine began howling his names, inside the house and then outside and then inside again—they stampeded.

Although Judy hadn't picked enough berries for three people, she returned to the house. On the lawn, the elegance of the enormous locust tree stopped her. Here in the shade she started to think about the painting she was working on in her studio— an emptied room on the second floor. Her canvas and still-life arrangement waited. Sometimes she would go to it and work and sometimes not. Her life wasn't easy.

From down the driveway came a sound like a gust of wind in the trees. She'd heard that noise often enough, waiting for her husband's car to return from the city. When someone really came she always knew for sure. Thinking this car must be Jonathan's mother, she crouched down on the lawn and put her hands over her ears.

"Get up," Catherine's stern voice ordered. "The whole town will think we're mad," she said, as Judy peeked up. Judy remembered, looking at the fierce tendon at the back of Catherine's ankle, how her own mother used to punish her by making her kneel on rice. "Slovenly child!" her mother bellowed at her the time she'd left a soaked Kleenex from a bloody nose on the sink in the bathroom. Her mother had taken her into the kitchen and handed Judy newspaper to spread on the floor. When her mother finished sprinkling rice on the paper, she made Judy kneel and recite Hail Marys. Later her mother told her it was time to get up. But Judy hadn't the strength to move or ask for help. She had fallen down onto the paper and remained like a cat sitting in its litter until her father or uncle came back home and helped her up. The rice had left indentations in her knees that she felt with her finger under the covers at night. In the morning, when she put on the knee socks that went with her uniform, she had been horrified because her socks wouldn't stay high enough to cover the bruises.

"There are enough here to feed only one," Catherine commented, inspecting the raspberries. Judy looked at Catherine's tanned, handsome face with freckles and at Catherine's gold-gray hair pinned back by her ears. Until this thing about having a baby had come up, Judy had admired Catherine. For Catherine was well traveled, voiced opinions about politics, finished the crosswords—pigging them—and corrected Judy's grammar: that is *he*, not *him*. Judy had never understood why Jonathan had divorced Catherine and couldn't picture what horrible thing had happened to Catherine to make her consider coming to live with her ex-husband and Judy, who had at the time been Jonathan's young bride. Judy wouldn't have done such a thing.

Judy still heard wheels on the gravel as she remained crouched on the ground. Catherine raised Judy's chin up with the fuzzy slipper and pointed to Jim, the farmer next door, driving his tractor up the driveway. He wore a yellow raincoat and a gas mask and aimed a hose from which a weed-killing solution sprayed.

"The whole town will think we're mad," Catherine repeated, waving at Jim, who had, ever since Jonathan moved in, been paid for doing all the work on the farm.

The word *mad* had a peculiar intensity for Catherine. She thought she was one of the few who could say what mad was and yet know that she herself was sane. Bending down, Catherine grabbed a weed from a periwinkle patch surrounding the base of the tree. Judy had risen and was sitting cross-legged back against the trunk. Catherine watched a beetle leap from the upheld root in her hand. As it fell, she remembered mad: herself in the white gown, a somnambulist walking from the hospital into the streets of New Delhi with the intravenous needle stuck in her arm, the tubes trailing. Silly thing, what had she been doing? After the divorce and a satisfactory settlement, she'd quit her job with the radio station and, because she'd always wanted to do it, traveled to India. After a year of traveling—six months of which she had spent on an unresolvable affair with an American doctor doing research there—she had come down with amoebic dysentery. Delirious in the Indian hospital, she had hallucinated. It seemed to her that voices from another life guided her. The unfamiliar doctors told her she was having psychotic episodes. When it was clear she would not die, she was sent back to Toronto.

Soon after that Catherine had arrived at the farm in Collingwood, two hours north of Toronto, where she'd heard Jonathan had moved with his new wife. Having himself heard about Catherine's sickness, Jonathan had told Catherine she could stay for a time, thinking too, Judy knew, that Catherine would be good company for his wife whenever he was away. So Catherine had arrived with her yellow suitcases, her hair swept up like a debutante's to cover the top that had not completely grown back after her illness, and parked her VW so that it blocked the driveway. She had brought a bottle of cognac and kissed Judy as though they were old friends. Thirty years old at the time, Judy stepped back cautiously. But she accepted the gift, knowing it had been bought with money Jonathan regularly sent Catherine—because he had to. Catherine instructed Jonathan to take her on "le grand tour." Earlier Jonathan had warned Judy about Catherine's irritating lapses into French.

After Jonathan had brought Catherine's suitcases to her room and then taken her off on the grand tour of the farm, Judy had searched through all of Catherine's things, her dresses, lotions, books, shoes. In the arms of an old cashmere sweater, Judy had come across a black-and-white photograph of Catherine in India. Catherine wore a white hospital gown. Her hair had thinned. She had lost so much weight the shape of her skull across the brow came through as in an X ray. Her pupils were enlarged; her look was desperate, babyish. Her skin looked rough and spotted like that of a woman dying of old age. Judy had put the photograph back in the arms of the sweater and had left the room wondering if Catherine were Catholic too.

"It'll be impressive serving berries for tea," Catherine told Judy, putting the container down on Judy's legs, which were stretched out in front of her now.

"She didn't say for sure she was coming for tea, did she? What if she comes for dinner?"

"In either case, those won't be enough berries," Catherine said, and then headed back toward the house.

Judy got up and ran through the rough grass in her plastic sandals. She stopped to watch a bird hopping on the ground underneath a lopsided apple tree. Always short of breath, not athletic like Catherine, she saw the bird lift a worm from the ground. And then suddenly she was outside a door watching Catherine eat; Catherine was opening her mouth and chewing so that Judy could see inside: roast beef. Judy wanted to run as the bird flew off, but remembered to be careful. An accident could ruin her life.

Before she'd met Jonathan, she'd been walking down Yonge Street in Toronto one day wearing white go-go boots when she had tripped off the curb and broken her ankle. It was during her first year at York University—one of the few times she'd been east of British Columbia. Sent home in a cast to recover, she had lost her first bit of freedom. Her mother, who was sixty years old, tried to cheer her up by playing Peter, Paul, and Mary songs on the old upright. Judy had turned up the volume on the game shows. Those days her mother sold Mary Kay cosmetics, and by the time she finished each day, both Judy's father and uncle, whom Judy remembered fondly for their faith in her, had returned from the shipyards and begun decorating every flat surface of the house with beer bottles. At home she'd felt plain and poor. Her mother no longer punished Judy, although she came out of her room periodically complaining about this and that in a shrill voice, shaking one of her many high-heeled shoes. Certain now that her mother would not hit her, Judy encouraged her mother to get out of the house, and so when she came back from one of the Mary Kay parties, Judy had felt obligated to ask how many blushers she had sold. Her uncle and father told Judy daily how much they loved her. They counted on her for bailing them out in their old age and beamed while reciting the story about the day the letter came announcing her scholarship. She had

resolved during those months, when they told her—repeatedly—
that they would hold off buying a dishwasher to pay for her
flight back to Toronto, to do something big with her life.

But her ankle had never healed properly. Back in Toronto without
the cast she went again and again to her orthopedic surgeon, Jonathan Edwards, whom four years later she married. They had six
years together before Catherine came to live with them. Two years
after that, Jonathan had fallen through the ice and been killed.

There was another bird in front of Judy. It nodded its head,
pick-pecked, fluttered, fluttered, danced, dipped, flew away when
a rabbit bounded near. Sensing Judy suddenly, the rabbit froze.
Its ears, she noticed, were orange and flickered lightly; it was
as though a monarch butterfly sat weightlessly on its head. She
moved back slowly to release the rabbit. Judy too sometimes froze
out of fear. She watched the rabbit flip its legs, thinking that she
must remember to notice Catherine that way. Something about
Catherine made Judy afraid to look. For a long time she believed
the photograph of Catherine in India was of that woman's soul.

Judy picked the raspberries without stopping now. Though a
bee landed on her nose and scared her, she finished by shaking
the container to level off the berries and peered in with satisfac-
tion. There were enough for Jonathan's mother to have a bowlful,
drowned with cream.

Judy walked toward the house. Opening the front door, she
paused to listen. Then she began singing Catherine's name
throughout the downstairs, meaning to be praised for the mound
of berries. She wondered if she should have tried to surprise
Catherine. Maybe if she found her off guard, they would laugh
together as they had that morning, dancing for rain. And so she
sneaked upstairs and threw open Catherine's bedroom door and
saw her, one breast fallen over in a strange position, her large
nipple swollen, almost bleeding as though a child had been sucking, sucking. Had Catherine done this to herself? They were
large enough. The other breast was partly hidden, her legs wound
tightly in the sheet and quilt. Catherine's mouth, stuck in a yawn,
blew heavy breaths forth like tiny grunts. A moth flicked its wings

on the reading light above Catherine's face, illuminated and flushed. Shutting the door, Judy went to her studio, where she stared at the still-life arrangement she'd been organizing for days.

She sat quietly for several moments looking at the objects: the cast-iron frying pan, the dried flowers lying flat. Then she heard Catherine scream. Now is the time to tell her, Judy thought, rushing in. She began to form the words: "No, I will never have a child with you." But when she saw Catherine fully awake and already half composed, she changed her mind.

"Has she come?" Catherine asked.

"No, no, not yet."

Catherine got up, brushed her hair, powdered under her arms and at her crotch so that the room filled with lily of the valley. She put on a linen dress with a low-cut back and looked fresh. Next, Judy showed Catherine the berries, and Catherine kissed her in a sisterly way on the side of Judy's lips.

"Have you noticed," Judy asked her, "how pregnant Molly is?" The cat sat at the threshold of the door, its belly drooping like an extra chin. Catherine stopped to pet the cat, jealously, jealously.

Judy went downstairs and soaped and resoaped her hands; they were never quite free from paint. She dried them and began soaping them again when Catherine came into the kitchen carrying a bunch of lilies. After putting them in water, Catherine tried to pry the closed ones open.

"I'll get headaches if you bring boarders here."

"You're a hypochondriac. Jonathan even said so."

"I'm an artist. He used to say that too."

"Why don't you ever take your canvases outside then?" Catherine, who had ripped apart one lily, decided to leave the others. She always asked Judy that.

"He liked my work, didn't he? He told you that?"

"Of course he did," Catherine answered directly.

"Nothing." She had spoken softly as though Catherine had asked her what she was thinking, and then started to lather up her hands again.

"You'll help when there are guests, won't you, dear?" Catherine handed her the towel. "The money will pay Jim's salary next month."

"He deserves more than that," Judy answered. "Do you know he even cut down the dead sycamores along the field across the road?"

"We'll pay him more then."

"You tend to be cheap," Judy told her.

"The house is in her name. What if she wants it? Where will we go? We'll need money."

"None of that is upon us yet," Judy had answered.

"He didn't leave a fortune."

"He left plenty," Judy insisted.

"Do you or do you not want to have children?"

"I never think about it," Judy answered.

Catherine stared at Judy so long that Judy turned her eyes, and when she stayed in that position Catherine suddenly lunged at her. With one big hand on each of Judy's shoulders, she shook Judy so that Judy's head flopped up and down.

"Jonathan's dead." Catherine spat out the words.

"Not that dead," Judy answered.

"But I had a dream the other day," Catherine persisted more quietly. "You don't understand. I dreamed that Jonathan drowned with my child inside him."

Judy reached up into the cupboard above the sink, brought out a box of rice, and began to sprinkle it over a small area on the tile. Then she bent over and folded her pants up above her small knees.

"I've always wondered if it would still hurt," Judy explained to Catherine as she knelt down on the kernels.

"I'm trying to tell you that I can never have children. It's too late for me."

"You tell me that every day, sometimes ten times a day," Judy responded, adjusting her position on the rice, closing her eyes. Catherine was supposed to be the stronger one. "Will we stay together?" Judy asked helplessly, opening her eyes.

"I don't know what will happen. It depends on what his mother

says when she comes," Catherine responded toughly, knowing
Judy wanted her to say—yes, of course, forever. That's the way
Judy was.

"It does. It still hurts!"

"Then get up. Get up!" She pulled Judy to her feet, hugging
her without restraint.

❖   ❖   ❖

Later in the afternoon, Judy fetched a decoy. Made over into an
ashtray, the wooden duck from the living room fit into the still-
life she'd been plotting for days. After staring at the arrangement
with the new object in place, she changed the position of the
chunky kitchen knife. She'd used it in other paintings. The glass
of water, she pushed back. She was interested here in painting
different weights and so had chosen some light things such as a
scarf and the dried flowers and heavier ones like the cast-iron
frying pan, new. Something was missing. She needed to finish
off the scene. Walking the halls of the second floor she noticed
Catherine's yellow suitcases lined up neatly against a papered
wall. In the bathroom down the hall she saw the fluffy brown
bath mat lying like a vast cow pie in the center of the white tile.
When she stood still to listen, she heard from downstairs the
noise of the small hand-held vacuum cleaner and knew for sure
that Catherine was using it to suck up dead flies along the win-
dowsills. Judy had known for some time that the noise of the
miniature vacuum reminded Catherine of the loud hum the machine made during her abortion many years ago. Over and over
Judy had offered to take care of the flies when Catherine was out
shopping so that Catherine wouldn't have to hear it. Just then the
noise stopped. Judy again scanned the bathroom for another
object she could use in her still-life and then remembered the
time Catherine had come back from town several weeks ago with
meat from the butcher. For some reason, Catherine had brought
the meat upstairs to the bathroom, where Judy was cleaning her
ears with a Q-tip. Catherine had left the roast on the sink, bleed-

ing through the brown paper. Dipping one end of the cotton into the blood, Judy had begun to paint on the mirror.

"They think we're lesbians," Catherine had told Judy. "The butcher implied it."

"Who does?" Judy asked.

"It'd be convenient if we were, wouldn't it?" Catherine had smoothed out the fringe of the mat with her toes.

Judy remembered having thought that Catherine's tone had been dishonest when she'd said it'd be more convenient if they were lesbians. It wasn't true, Catherine had no interest. Judy had wondered, looking at Catherine in a sexual way, feeling sexual as she often did now that it had been so long, if she could. Catherine would have to be different, she supposed. But the sun had been shining on Catherine that day through the bathroom window. Reflecting off the tile it had shot up Catherine's legs so that Judy couldn't see her very well. A dead fly had fallen onto the floor, dropping from nowhere. Catherine had picked it up with her fingers. Standing, she had looked carefully at the mirror.

"You can paint a bird," Catherine had commented.

"Do you realize birds spend all of their time looking for food?" Judy had replied, putting the last touches—segments—on a worm.

"If only our lives were that simple." Catherine had sighed and rubbed her belly, Judy remembered.

Backing away from the bathroom slowly, Judy now considered the oil lamp on the hall table, a needlepoint doorstop, a tube of toothpaste, a candle sitting on the toilet top that Catherine lit sometimes to cover up odor—her stomach hadn't been right since India. As Judy was standing in the hall, the lights suddenly went dim. The power had been getting less strong all week, throughout the heat wave. The ice cubes wouldn't freeze anymore, and only a yellow glow came from a 100 watt bulb. Not enough light to paint by. She gave up her search and went downstairs to find Catherine.

"Dinner for three, n'est-ce pas? She should be here soon, don't you think?" They both nodded as though agreeing on something very important.

Catherine took the chicken out of the freezer, and Judy noticed that it was already mostly thawed. They sat down together and waited for it to loosen utterly. One hour went. Another. The plate of tea cookies was gone. At nine o'clock his mother hadn't arrived.

"She used to send me checks when I was head of fund-raising for CPR," Catherine bragged. Judy had heard the story before, and she also knew that Catherine hadn't been on good terms with his mother since Catherine's abortion. According to Jonathan, during dinner one night at Jonathan's mother's house, Catherine had blurted out, as though proud of her independent stance on the issue, that she'd had an abortion against Jonathan's will. Jonathan had rescued the conversation, but from then on there had been no more dinner invitations, no more checks for the radio station, nor friendly phone calls to her daughter-in-law's office.

Catherine had taken his mother's rejection hard. She hated herself too: spreading before a doctor, a white mask over his nose and mouth, and then being entered by the machine. The pain revealed to her that the abortion had been a mistake. Now when she sucked up the flies, once, sometimes twice, a day, she remembered all of it. Damn those flashes through her thighs and upward!

Judy then told Catherine that she would probably sit and finish her mystery novel or go watch *The Ghost and Mrs. Muir.* Catherine got up to fill a bottle with a sponge on top and shuffled to the office to wet stamps, leaving Judy with the chicken, which had thawed.

Judy put her entire hand on the back of the chicken for a minute. Then she washed and dried the hand. Turning the water off, she listened for a car. Judy looked down at the table and dusted cookie crumbs onto the floor, noticing then the completed crossword. The word *yo-yo* stuck out. She doubted whether it was two words, but she was thinking instead about how she would finish her painting.

As Judy sat, she pressed one hand with the other into a fist and then reversed this motion. When the lights began to flicker, she stopped. Then the lights faded and were gone. A blackout. Judy heard nothing from the room where Catherine was; presumably she could lick stamps in the dark. Waiting for the noise of her obscene slippers, Judy suddenly felt fond of Catherine. Jonathan's mother and indeed Jonathan had no right to expect a child, to expect anything. The bay was clearer to Judy with the inside lights out. From the size of the waves, always different, she could tell exactly the mood of the wind. She saw constellations she knew the names of. He had taught them to her. Judy began to name the stars out loud as surely as she could name the provinces. Orion, the Big and Little Dippers, Scorpius. It reassured her to say concrete things like what day it was. The Evening Star had been big with Jonathan. He used to say it represented constancy, their love. Even with Catherine in the room, he had come up to her and put his arms around her—Judy. Catherine, Judy remembered, had wanted to save the soggy skates.

"She's here," Catherine whispered, coming up behind.

"You scared me," Judy said with a slight scream in her voice. "I can't see anything."

"Come with me." Catherine took Judy's hand confidently, as though it wasn't at all dark, and led her to the master bedroom, where Judy still slept at night. Judy heard the car door slam.

"Get under the bed with me," Catherine told her in a loud whisper. "Get under quick before she comes in and hears us."

Judy didn't move.

"If she doesn't see us, she might forget about us. She doesn't need this place. She hates flies."

"How do you know?"

"Hurry, get under." Catherine, who was already lying flat under the bed, pulled at Judy's ankle. "Get under, dammit."

Slowly Judy followed her under the bed, and Catherine took her hand. Together they listened to his mother knock and enter.

"Her couches are peach colored with tiny upraised dots," Catherine whispered.

"Like the skin of the chicken?" Judy answered.

Jonathan's mother called hello in the ringing way rich people do, like saying yellow, making themselves in any case sound foreign. Judy heard that. Catherine heard her own mother. Holding Judy's hand tighter, Catherine was attracted to the way his mother sang hello. They should have prepared the chicken tetrazzini, opened a bottle of wine, set the table. It could have been like the old days. Why hadn't they pretended nothing was wrong?

"Whisper," Judy demanded. His mother didn't know the house well, and they heard her bump into things. When Jonathan had wanted to move his practice away from Toronto to the country, his mother had resolved her disappointment by being especially generous: she had bought him this farmhouse.

"It's hot under here," Judy said.

"Maybe it will rain finally," Catherine answered. They heard her footsteps downstairs.

"Remember when you clipped off Jonathan's mustache?" Catherine asked.

"I wanted to see his whole face. 'Think how I would hate touching that hair over your lip if I were blind,' I told him. He agreed to let me snip it. Some of the hair went up his nose, and I couldn't stop laughing."

"The nurses he worked with thought you were trying to keep the competition away," Catherine laughed softly. Quickly, though, her voice flattened. "But you were never that way about men. I'm not going to have an easy time finding you one."

They listened to the footsteps.

"Do you think Jonathan left us alone too much? In the winter he was at the hospital all the time—all those stupid skiers breaking their legs."

"Yes, I used to think he did leave me alone," Judy answered.

"Did you hate being left alone with me?" Catherine persisted.

"No."

"Why didn't you go with him when he traveled?"

"My painting. You always forget how important my painting is."

"I went to a medical conference with Jonathan once in east Africa when we were first married."

Downstairs they heard a dish break.

"In east Africa, I had nothing to do, so I went to shops. I didn't buy any ivory because of the elephants, poor things. I went to the tearooms, though, and ordered passion-fruit juice and sat down beside a small black woman to drink my juice and write in my diary. The woman spoke pretty good English and told me she knew a woman who was on trial for stealing another woman's pregnancy."

"Shhh," Judy said, listening to the footsteps.

"The Kikuyu recognize tribal law."

"What are you getting at?"

"Some women will do anything to have a child."

Feeling a bit claustrophobic, Judy wished the bedspread didn't hang down to the floor, hiding them completely.

"Anything?" she said.

"A pregnant woman woke up one morning and was no longer pregnant. Later she heard that her neighbor, who everyone knew to be barren, was jumping up and down for joy because finally, at age forty-five, she was pregnant. The first woman accused the second of putting a curse on her doorstep—in legal terms, of stealing her pregnancy."

Judy didn't say anything for a minute. She let the silence frighten them, and then she spoke harshly, "No one *stole* your pregnancy. Why did you have an abortion if you didn't want it? And why did you go to India? You do things of your own free will and then complain when they go all wrong."

"At least I have a free will," Catherine whispered back.

Judy thought about this for a minute. It was true in a way. She struggled to take initiative with her painting and let other things go as they would. Left alone, it wouldn't have occurred to her to have some man's child. On the other hand, a part of her challenged Catherine to convince her to do it.

"Why doesn't she go?" Judy asked. She didn't want to fight. Catherine would never admit now that Judy did have a free will. When Catherine made a mistake, Judy thought, she simply came back at whatever it was in a different way, making excuses. Catherine didn't give up.

"Remember when Jonathan used to tease you about your ankle, imitating what a great faker you'd been? You used to laugh so hard. I'd never seen you laugh like that. They're pretty now, your ankles are."

"So are yours," Judy responded, thinking how really funny Jonathan had been when he imitated the way she had limped in order to prolong her visits to his office.

"Listen, I hear your name. She's calling your name, and her voice sounds weird like she's never said it before. She must realize something's happened to the power."

"I can tell exactly where she is because of those high heels."

"In the kitchen now," Catherine said.

"Like a cow wearing a bell," Judy thought out loud.

"She's wonderfully built."

"I thought you hated her."

They then heard his mother open the kitchen door, which led onto the porch in the back of the house, facing the bay. There was more light out there than inside, Judy knew, thinking of the stars. They heard her call in the direction of where Jonathan had the accident, probably cupping her hands over her mouth. "Ladies," she called.

"If we had a child—if *you* did—we could bring her up to be a painter like you," Catherine said.

"Ladies," they heard her call again, her word hit by the wind. Judy remembered how she had stood with her out on the slate beach, then pocked with snow, and watched the boat attempt to dredge Jonathan up. It had taken all day.

"He was a great skater," his mother had said to Judy, and Judy had noticed as she spoke how the neck of her black dress overflowed under her chin.

"There's the puck." Judy had pointed to a patch of ice beyond the spot where Jonathan had fallen through. "The puck he was chasing after," she had explained, just as the boat, fishing for his body, plunged through many more feet of ice. Judy and his mother had seen the boat plow over the puck, and Judy had

stood in front of her and cried while Jonathan's mother gripped
the wooden railing and shook a post loose.

There was another noise downstairs—maybe his mother was
helping herself to raspberries or kicking the cat. Judy thought
about her still-life again and then felt Catherine's knee nod against
her own. Judy noticed Catherine now, now that she couldn't see
her, now that the sun wasn't in the way: Judy noticed all at once
all the little things about Catherine—the kinds of things that had
enabled her to love Jonathan too. Judy wondered then if she
hadn't expected Jonathan's death all along, as if it were part of
the sadness she had always, especially as a child, carried with
her.

"Answer me." A cupboard slammed and his mother was in
another room shouting at them. "Answer me!" The two women
moved even closer together, and Catherine touched Judy's ear
with two fingers as though it were something odd and interesting, as though the feeling she created would inspire in Judy a
response.

"Will we stay together?" Judy asked.

"Don't ask that," Catherine ordered.

"You want a child to absorb our suffering. What will happen
to the man?"

"Nothing," Catherine answered, confused.

"I mean, will the man stay around?"

"It doesn't matter," Catherine said more confidently.

Judy took her hand away from Catherine's. Holding such a
thing was no longer comforting.

"What I mean is, it would depend on whether we like him
enough, or whether he wants to stay."

Judy's spine butted the hardwood floor. It hurt. She wanted to
roll away from Catherine. She wondered why she didn't have the
strength to call out, "We're here, under the bed." She wanted to
run downstairs and appeal to his mother. His mother would
surely interfere, take away the house so that Judy could start a
new life, unattached. But Catherine was whispering something,

and it was hard to concentrate—she let her thoughts drift away as though they were only a part of a dream. She wasn't in control anyway.

"You're lucky you're still young." Catherine practically sang this information, and Judy struggled to listen instead to the snooping-around noises his mother was making downstairs. Would she come upstairs?

"Jonathan told me you're talented, Judy. I always believed him. I believe in you." Judy heard his mother's footsteps at the bottom of the stairs, and she prayed she would come up, find them, and change everything. His mother might easily discover them under the bed, if Judy would only stick her foot out from under the spread. Carefully, over the course of several minutes, Judy did this. She left her foot exposed so that if his mother came upstairs she would discover them. Judy imagined his mother spotting the foot from the door; her strong hand with rings on at least two fingers would reach under the bed to help Judy out. But, although Judy steepled her hands to enforce this wish, she didn't have the strength to move or call for help.

Inside the closet, Molly, without uttering a sound, her hind legs spread, the area behind widened, burst forth onto the pile of towels. Judy thought there was an odor in the room. She reached down her own leg and lightly pressed the bruises below her knees.

Outside the sound of the car engine blocked the confusion caused by a breeze. Then came—and to both of them it was a good omen—the sudden slapping of rain hitting the dry leaves and grass. Under the bed their breathing was louder than the short licks made by the mother cat.

"She's gone," Catherine giggled, sliding out.

Koh Samui

"Look at number nine," he said, reading from the sheet of paper he had just unwrapped from a small brown bottle. "'Bloody, bloody: for female only' it says." He pried off the plastic lid, which popped like a champagne cork, and took a timid swig.

"That's not the one you chose, is it?" she asked.

"Guess," he replied, handing her the sheet on which the ten kinds of Thai herbal whiskey were neatly typed. She put the list up to the kerosene lamp that only dimly illuminated the porch of their beach bungalow and glanced at the different kinds he could have chosen: Good Health, Spiritual Awakening, Sex Appeal. . . . The paper almost blew out of her hands in the strong wind. She knew which one he'd picked.

"How's it taste?" she asked.

He made a face, but took another swallow.

"You'd hate it," he said, handing her the bottle. She sniffed it, put her feet up on the railing, and leaned back in the sturdy bamboo chair. "Imperial Hotel, same chairs," the bungalow owner told them at lunch. "Here, 150 baht a night; there 2,500 baht a night. Why American people go?" Allison had shrugged her shoulders and told him his bungalows were the most beautiful on the island. From two of the three bedroom windows they had a view of the ocean. Even now in the dark they were so close they could see the six tiers of waves breaking almost simultaneously. The sound still kept them awake at night.

"You'd have been fine, you know, once we got on the main road."

"It's three miles to the main road, Ted," she said, and held up her arm, which was deeply scratched, the dried blood still unwashed. She hadn't gone with him that afternoon to the fishing village where he found the Thai whiskey because when she first turned the hand throttle just a bit to test it, her bike had sped forward and hit three bumps; she avoided a coconut tree by skidding sideways, and the cycle fell on top of her. The Thai men and women who had been watching the lesson, and Ted, huddled around her. There was laughter underneath their concern. With a great deal of grace, she thought, she smiled at everyone, even Ted, and retreated to the bungalow to read. The motorbike was an enemy. Her husband roared off on his own.

"Did you guess yet?" he asked.

She looked at him, but didn't answer. The new golden mustache he'd begun when they left the U.S. was fully grown—it added an elegant flourish to his profile.

"He's sweeping again," Ted said. Allison turned her head to watch the tall man in red briefs whisk sand from the steps of the bungalow he shared with a younger man, whose head was shaved close around the ears and dyed a coarse blond on top. Like mimes, the two Frenchmen had drawn a circle around themselves, an invisible bubble, and none of the guests dared violate it. Through the protection of dark glasses, Allison had finally glimpsed what each was reading on the beach, and it confirmed her impression that the older one was some kind of intellectual, the younger one not. That afternoon the younger one had brought a large mirror onto the porch and lathered up his face before shaving. Meanwhile, the older one, the one who appealed to Allison, was lying full-out like a bronze statue on the wet sand while the waves, a mere whisper then, licked at his body. She walked back and forth several times along that section of the beach in order to look at him and then suddenly began pretending she'd all along been looking for shells. The younger man had seen her.

"Have you noticed the two American women in bungalow six?"

"Have I noticed?" Ted answered in a mocking voice.

"I mean the way they talk."

The tiny bikini bottoms they wore on the beach rode high over their hipbones and firm bottoms. They stretched their limbs together on their towels and executed graceful one-handed cartwheels—though, Allison noted to Ted, they always did them downhill.

"How do they talk?" he asked.

"Apparently the owner's brother, the one who takes food orders—you know, he wears the Bob Marley T-shirt . . ."

"The Babylon By Bus tour—1978."

"He asked the redheaded one if he could have her linen shirt."

"Did she give it to him?" Ted asked.

"That's when I heard the redhead say to her friend: 'Can you believe it, I mean like he actually asked could he have it, and I'm like, excuse me?'"

Ted laughed at Allison's perfect imitation of the way the young women spoke.

"It's the voice of collegiate America. They're sorority sisters, University of Virginia."

"It's something else too," she said, and turned a page in her book.

"Did you read the section on Krabi yet?"

"I think I'd rather go north to Chiang Mai. The beaches are so full of tourists."

"We're tourists."

"We're travelers," she insisted, and repeated their itinerary so far: India, Nepal, Malaysia, Burma, Thailand.

"We're honeymooners," he said, grinning.

"It's such a dumb word."

"That's why I like it."

Allison didn't say anything.

"Hey listen," Ted said, "it's done. You traded in a big fancy wedding for this."

"I don't regret it," she said. "Do you?"

"But you still feel guilty, taking the money from your parents."

"Can you see me in one of those white numbers?"

"I'd rather see you in one of those topless bathing suits. Allison, you're the only one . . ."

"Right. So you're against going hiking in Chiang Mai?"

"I could easily stay *here* until we go to China, store energy like a lizard." Ted spread his arms out as if to embrace the night. It was then that Allison noticed the ghostly figure of a woman on the wet rocks. During the day, the rocks were covered with water. Although the tide was now way down, it seemed to Allison a melodramatic place for anyone to sit in the dark.

"It's weird, isn't it, how most of the women on the beaches here have really terrific bodies. It makes me a little uncomfortable," she said in a more intimate voice than she'd used with him since her spill.

"Libraries attract good minds; beaches are for beautiful bodies."

"Where do you fit in?" she snapped. It always made her angry, the way he reduced things. So pat, so singsong. Sometimes she thought that impulse would make him an accomplished journalist. Other times, she thought nobody would hire a man who wrote like that: "and then everybody gets porridge." Ted was the first to admit that his high marks in journalism school were partly due to her. She read all his work carefully. "Make your endings less conclusive," she often told him. "Let the reader decide." She corrected his spelling, even his grammar.

Once, during that time—they were graduate students in different programs living together in Somerville, Massachusetts—he'd gotten up in the middle of the night and stood by the window. Somehow, missing the warmth of his body, she'd woken up too and seen him standing there, one strong leg up on a stool as though it were a rock and he was a man surveying his land: the things he owned. In great seriousness, he apologized to her for being such a maverick. Why? Because it had taken him so long to commit himself to her? Of course she understood that he was apologizing for his affair with Carolyn. Allison hadn't made fun of him for calling himself a maverick then, but realized that she would have now.

The sound of singing came from the bungalow across from

theirs. Da-ta-ta-tas and la-la-la-las. It stopped and there was laughter. A moment later an older French couple walked toward Allison and Ted. The woman wore a shawl. They were on their way to dinner.

"Bon soir," they said in unison. The man had his arm around his wife and was smiling absurdly. Allison had watched them, too, that afternoon, splashing together in the water.

"He's teaching her how to do breaststroke," Ted said after they'd gone on. Allison thought to herself how pleasant it would be to be like that when she and Ted were old. She leaned her head back, looked up at the stars, and laughed at herself: "and then everybody gets porridge."

"I can't quite picture her squatting. Can you?" Allison asked.

"That's why most older people don't stay here. They like to sit on the can with a magazine."

"You have to admit it's strange though, the way the European women walk around so casually, even the old ones."

"The cartwheel sisters go topless too, and they're Americans."

"I know, but they're just showing off."

Allison and Ted were both looking at the woman on the rocks. Allison spoke next in a voice she saved for poetry:

> But th'other rather higher did arise,
> And her two lily paps aloft displayed
> And all, that might his melting hart
>   entice
> To her delights, she unto him
>   betrayed:
> The rest hid underneath, him more
>   desirous made.

"Who's that?" Ted asked cautiously.

"Spenser."

"I love it that you're literary."

"But?"

"Well, what's the point?"

"You stare at them," Allison told him flatly.

Ted laughed and reached for Allison's hand.

"I mean," she said, "they're not really erotic in this context, are they?"

"And the Thais—have you seen them?—swim with all their clothes on."

"What's it mean?" she asked him.

"It's colonialism in reverse: the Europeans are going native."

Allison shook her head and rolled her eyes in playful disgust.

"I think I'll have the curried shark tonight," Ted told her, looking happy at the prospect. He picked up a small rock from the porch and threw it hard. She was sure he'd made it to the water.

"Do you see her down there on the boulder?"

"Who?" Allison asked. It was the first time in the three days they'd been on Koh Samui that either one had made a direct reference to the Swiss woman. Normally, Allison and Ted discussed everyone.

"She reminds me of Carolyn," he said, putting one of his golden legs on the railing. Allison said nothing. Ted hadn't mentioned Carolyn's name in almost two years. Allison knew how to handle this. Say nothing. And later, at dinner, say nothing. She would answer his questions. Make this or that remark about the food. It would take him some time to realize she'd withdrawn.

"I think I'll order the Thai salad," she said as she turned on the porch light and brought her guidebook to Thailand up as though she were reading it.

Ted continued to stare out at the beach. The Swiss woman was taking off her sarong. It flapped in the wind, and they watched her secure it with a rock before she slipped gracefully into the water. If only she spoke the woman's language, Allison thought, she would find some way to make her seem silly, insubstantial. Allison looked down at her book.

"My God," Ted said, standing.

Allison looked up and saw movement in the water beyond the breaking waves. It was astonishingly bright.

"Her body's on fire under the water."

"That's impossible," Allison laughed. For a moment she too was swept away by the sparkling image.

"You see it, don't you? Her whole body's glowing."

"A regular miracle," Allison then whispered so that Ted couldn't hear. She sat back down. As if to punish herself for wanting a minute before to fault the woman, Allison allowed Ted to be amazed at the apparition—his angel. Ted's face when he turned around to share his excitement with her was like a child's.

"Why don't you go see?" Allison said, feeling sure he would have gone down to the beach on his own. She tried hard to seem easygoing, and it was for that reason Allison yesterday had locked herself in the bathroom; she didn't want to be the one who waited anxiously for sex, and so she fixed it sometimes so he would have to wait.

"Ted," Allison called out a minute later. She didn't like him walking on the wet rocks. He looked back at Allison, and she flung her arm out, motioning him to return. In not too long, he did.

"It's something that happens in tropical waters," Allison explained, "phosphorescence. Melville wrote about it, or Conrad," she said drifting off a bit, trying to remember more precisely.

"After dinner, let's try it," he said. Allison shrugged, remembering her resolve to be cool, and skipped to a section on malaria and then, further on in the book, to one on Buddhism. She'd already asked Ted what he thought about doing a stint as a monk.

"The Boss is showing a pirated Rambo video tonight."

Allison didn't respond.

"The Thais love Rambo."

"Why do you suppose?" she said flatly.

"Stallone kills lots of communists, for one. For another, it was filmed here in Thailand."

"Makes sense," she said, still turning pages.

"It's beautiful, really," he continued. "Rambo goes back to Vietnam and uses guerrilla tactics to do to the Russians what the Vietcong did to us."

"Why do you keep calling him Boss? His name is Jao."

"He's the owner; he likes being called 'Boss.'"

Allison shook her head.

"What's really bugging you?" he asked.

Allison shrugged.

"Come on. Something's eating you."

Allison looked out at the water and noticed that the Swiss woman had gone.

"Do you think I don't know," he said. "Do you think I don't know you still want to punish me? Why can't we at least talk about Carolyn?"

Allison got up and went inside the dark bungalow. She lay down on the bed, her face to the wall. How dare he break her privacy that way? A moment later she heard the door open. She felt him next to her. He took her hand. She didn't know what she would have done if he'd left her alone.

"He drank half this bottle for you," he said, lifting the Thai whiskey up so that she could see, using the third person as they sometimes did when the subject was difficult. She felt his breath on her forehead.

"I'm the one who should be drinking the 'Sex Appeal,'" she said, turning toward him with a tentative smile. He put his hand under her purple dress. "She's sorry," she added, taking up his third-person address, knowing that being sorry didn't change anything for her but feeling sure that it was what she wanted to say.

About Johanna

We used to say Johanna had been born in the monstrous barn between the hunchbacked hills. Long after government-planted spruce grew child size to replace the dying locust trees that lay sideways like giant bones, long after the big old barn had burned down, those who knew my sister still thought of her as that girl who was born in a barn, that girl who died in a barn.

When Johanna was five she swung firm from knotted ropes. The ropes dangled from wide beams in various places so that one could swing from the third level to the second and from the second to the first. Sometimes Johanna would swing without jumping and wait until the rope stopped dead; then she screwed her body quickly to the top of it. When she was seven she could move hand-over-hand across rafters toward a diagonal beam and shimmy its length to straddle a crossbeam sixty feet above bales of hay.

I admired Johanna's fearlessness from below. Andrew, who is the oldest and married now, ignored her when she sat on the high rafters of the barn until, his patience gone, he yelled, "You're going to fall someday and then you'll be sorry." I waited until she roller-coastered down on a wheel pulley, which fit onto a rope she'd stretched from a ceiling rafter to the bottom of the chicken coop. It was worth the wait to play with Johanna because she made up games for us: "When I roll down this hill I want you to cover me with hay and leave me to die. Ready, set, go!" I watched her spin down the hill on her side, her arms crisscrossing her chest like a professional ice-skater's, and when she reached the bottom, I covered her with hay. If I came back too soon to see if she was all right, Johanna accused me of wrecking the game. I used to tell Andrew that Johanna was religious in a way, and he argued that she was the world's last pagan.

"What does Johanna do in the barn by herself?" my mother asked me. I told her about walking on beams, about hiding places and trying stunts with no hands. After she asked about Andrew too she apologized for keeping me. The screen door, which had never kept flies from the house, slammed behind me. As I walked through weeds to the barn, burrs caught on to my socks. I always gasped at the first moment of barn air. Light from the door lit up pieces of dust the way a flashlight would. My sister's body, clenched onto a beam by the knees, with her brown arms hanging straight down, was almost unnoticeable. An insect on bark. But I saw her. I stared at Johanna until her knees began to slip and she pulled herself upright. Together we ran down to the small river that we had dammed up for wading at an elbow turn. She bet me my allowance she could catch a trout with her bare hands, and she did. I saw her snatch the fish with my own eyes. Andrew has never believed it.

In the winter we went to Collingwood for the skiing, and no one played in the barn when it was cold. When school let out in early June, we went back to Collingwood for longer periods of time because our father, in good weather, was willing to commute into the city. It took until midsummer for all the old hay to dry out in our barn, which was bigger, older, more rundown than any in the county; all the kids whose families came up from Toronto on weekends wanted to play in it.

When it was Johanna's turn one day to be Jailor, she captured all the players in the "Bad Boy" game, including me, and locked us in a storage room of the barn, the jail. Only Craig, a boy whose legs were already as big as a man's, was still at large. If Johanna could find Craig and tag him before he was able to circle back to release us from the storage room, she would win the game. Finally she saw Craig jump from the main floor to the lower level. To cut him off, from where she stood on the third level, she maneuvered along a two-inch-wide ledge to the top of the chicken coop and from there jumped twenty-five feet to the lowest floor and tagged Craig, who thought he was crouching invisibly. He was shocked speechless by how suddenly Johanna came on him. At first she couldn't stand; I told her not to walk on it.

The next day, when she was certain her leg was broken, she asked Mother to take her for X-rays. I was the only one who asked to sign the cast. One night Johanna made designs on it with black paint and Father told her, grinning and gesturing smoothly with his cigar, that she was odd. "You are an odd one," he said. That was the kind of pronouncement that our father, who is an architect, often made.

During the weekdays the three of us were locked in private school—Johanna and I at Bishop Strachan School for Girls, Andrew at UTS, a serious academic school for boys. Johanna was the type to skip school but did not. None of us did. We lived in an old Tudor house right in the city. My parents stacked our drawers with crayons, our shelves with books, our boxes with rockets and magic; our beds for a long time were made by Celia, who lived on the third floor. My mother used the room above the garage for her office. She had lots of plants in that room and a big drawing table and a velvet chair that she told me was for her clients. She liked the stool for herself. My mother called herself a businesswoman, but my father insisted on calling her an artist, though she told people that she hadn't picked up a brush in years.

We lived for the weekends and holidays. It wasn't just the skiing, or tobogganing after skiing all day, or building jumps and climbing up the hill after the tows had closed down and stealing signs that said Keep Ski Tips Up; it wasn't just the ponds with tadpoles and trout thrown in so that old fishing rods might finally get used, or climbing the mountain boulders wearing shoes with suckers on the bottom. There was a mystery there, and it had to do with the way Johanna led us. Now that she is gone, I wonder. Perhaps the power of my nostalgia makes the afterglow.

One of those winters, Johanna and Andrew broke bones at the

same time. They tucked from the top of the bluff. Crouching with their poles cocked back, they charged down the mountain. They turned only when the slope itself turned. Even from the chairlift I could see how much both wanted to be first. Downhill training was an ordeal that left my body in a panic. I never felt protected wearing a helmet. That day I'd volunteered to help the coach set up the gates, telling him that my skis weren't releasing properly. The prospect of getting wrapped around a tree was real to me, but not to them: Johanna was an athlete, and Andrew challenged her at anything. Straining now to watch them over my shoulder from the lift, I could see that they had reached the bottom at the same time. With ski racks, ski people buckling boots, and others standing in lift lines, there was no room to stop, and they skied into the cement triangle that stuck out from the restaurant. Johanna and Andrew were strung up in traction for months in the small county hospital, and from what I saw during the many times I visited them I don't think they made much progress at getting along. Andrew, who had broken both legs, watched television, while Johanna, with one leg broken in four places, seemed to do nothing. She told me she concentrated on healing herself. This sounded ridiculous to me until she was released several months before Andrew. I remember them lying on the trampled snow, with ankles and thighs wrenched in wrong directions. Johanna had reached over and put her leather glove in Andrew's mouth to stop the noise he made. She had put the other glove over her own eyes to stop people from staring.

A few years later, on the day Johanna was supposed to qualify for the Can-Am team, Andrew and I found her waxing her cross-country skis in the barn. She told us she did not want to be an amateur ski racer but only wanted to ski. Mother and Father shrugged their shoulders, though I knew they were disappointed. Andrew said, "You fool, you would have made it." I said nothing but was aware of how much I'd wanted my sister to be a champion. Everyone knew she could have been. I watched her torch the first layer of wax and then rub the bottom with her palm until the thin layer shone like a lit candle. From the doorway of the barn she snapped the skis on without acknowledging Andrew or me and pushed and glided, pushed and glided, then pushed, pushed, pushed with shorter thrusts up one of the hunch-backed hills, leaving us behind.

One evening after an entire day of packing a jump so that Johanna could try her first aerial somersault on skis, Johanna and Andrew decided to ski cross-country. It was dusk and only two days into a new year. They were already exhausted, but it was important, they explained to me, to go before the new snow grew old and slow. They got lost. Without the proper mittens Johanna's fingers went white, though of course she could not see that in the dark. Andrew held her fingers. They traded his mittens back and forth so that her fingers again felt the pain of the cold.

They skied over the cliff, they later told me, to avoid having to circle miles around. The snow was soft and deep enough, but Johanna's skis crossed during the jump and twisted when she landed so that the side of one ski slit the back of her ear. (Later I often noticed the odd welt the size of an index finger between her skull and ear and once asked permission to feel it.) The blood on the snow was soon covered by new snow. Their faces were wind scratched, with pincushion cheeks, their muscles like ropes stretched in tugs-of-war. And Johanna's hands and throat were frostbitten as she finally led the way home to the farm.

Toward midnight they saw Mr. Franklin's bull in a snowdrift, and then they saw the barn half lit up by the moon and half hidden by falling snow. Mother and Father were not home; they had been out on the Williamses' snowmobile looking for Johanna and Andrew. When my brother and sister walked in all soggy, I was fiddling with my new camera and had let the fire go out. The teakettle was whistling away its last drops of water, and white Christmas tree lights were on. The room was soft. Mist floated up from the floor. When the telephone rang, Father's voice contained all that might have been expressed in words about fear and care.

My parents were not big on reprimands, and in my family you

didn't even tell stories about what terrible thing happened to you that day at school. Sometimes, though, we listened to my parents compare uncomplimentary stories about their clients.

My sister was not fashionable. Even wearing a school tie, even with gold hair expensively cut and pulled back, sedition showed in her stance, in the untucked shirt, the slight crackling noise in her throat when she spoke her choppy sentences. When she didn't wear her school uniform, she wore a leather jacket with elaborate fringe open over a black T-shirt that was too small and emphasized her small hard breasts. I guessed, long before she told me, that she met Craig in the barn at night and he was touching them and she was touching his penis and already putting it inside and loving that she could make him move it her way.

Before dawn one night, Johanna and Craig were lying on barn boards lightly covered with hay when the floor fell through. Fifteen boards collapsed beneath them. They landed on more hay than they had been on. Though bruised, they laughed. The next day, on a raft at the bay, I saw them notice one another's bodies, but they did not touch. I heard her tell him she was not the same person outside the barn.

Andrew knew and was jealous because he had not yet done what she had about sex. For me it was an impossible thing. Thinking of sex made me want to play the piano, or pull weeds up from the vegetable garden. Now, the thought of barn boards falling makes me smile. But Andrew had whispered coarsely to me that they were just like wild animals. It was the type of judging statement Andrew liked to make. Those days he drank a lot of beer, sometimes with skiing buddies, sometimes with us in the barn. What startled me was learning that he followed Johanna and Craig down to the barn at night. It was dark, so he only listened from a small passageway. I found the place where he had crouched because change that had fallen from his pocket was still there the next day. There probably wasn't a lot for him to listen to, though. Barn creaking covered by older barn noises, a few quiet words and laughs muffled by distance, and a few small sounds from deep in the throats of the animals.

Craig wrote Johanna phrases, words, things he hoped she could not call sappy. I recognized one as a line from a D. H. Lawrence poem: "The pain of loving you is almost more than I can bear." When Johanna showed it to me, written inside a matchbook cover, she said it was meant to be sarcastic. I said that he was trying to sound like a man with a beard. For one year they saw each other every weekend and even more often during Christmas and summer holidays. Toward the end of the year he described her on paper as a tall golden wheat stalk, standing aloof. A month later she wrote to him for the first time: "It is your fault for not being what I need; it is my fault for not needing what you are." That was it. When Craig received those few melodramatic words he called our house in the city every half hour and managed to speak to Johanna because Father put the receiver in her hand. I saw from the living room. I then heard her laugh with Craig as easily as ever. I suppose, in the end, Craig said to her that she was silly, that there would not always be a barn and that they would have to see each other in the city, too.

When that never came about, Craig told Andrew that Johanna was a bitch. "Your sister is a goddamn bitch," he said. Andrew said, "She isn't. She's not the same. You changed her." The only place Craig had ever been with Johanna alone was in the barn, and when she would not see him even there, he knew it was over. Not long afterward, he was accepted at Berkeley and drove a motorcycle to the West Coast. Four years later he was drafted into the U.S. Army and was the only Canadian I knew killed in Vietnam.

Mom and Dad never gave her guidance. I was more demanding and probably more malleable. I spent most of my free time practicing the piano. It was Johanna who gave me the encouragement to play. I wanted her complicity, and I thought we understood each other because of all the times she stood by me when Andrew's big-deal friends pulled up my skirt or called me a girly girl. She chased them the way she used to chase the cows, landing on their backs with a thud. It was something to see her ride a cow.

Most of the time Johanna dealt with Andrew and me separately. Occasionally she noticed what went on between us. During a rainy, overlong week at Grandmother's island, called Rock Island—we called it Spook Island—Andrew and I fought. He was a popular king of the camp type who considered me morose because I got along with Johanna, gave piano recitals in the school auditorium, and wasn't a great ski racer.

What happened the day we rowed past the buoys tells something about him. It wasn't stormy but waves hit against each other. Andrew was bailing. I could feel Johanna watching from a boulder near the water. She sat cross-legged surrounded by blueberry plants. I saw her throw a rock at a water snake that humped its back as it moved through the outskirts of the water like an eel. I was at the oars, rowing toward the Ojibwa. The soothing double sound of the rowing motion accompanied the musical themes I played in my head. Andrew stood suddenly from the stern and demanded that I turn back.

I may have asked why. Or what was wrong. I couldn't see any reason to turn back. There wasn't one. When Andrew realized I wasn't following his orders, he stood, moved toward me, and shook me. Stunned, I didn't resist his claws pinching blood from my shoulders. I screamed. Andrew swung his fist into my open mouth. I didn't fall out of the boat, but the force and the angle of the jab threw me off balance. I relinquished the oars and sat back, saying over and over again, "I can't believe you did that." Andrew couldn't believe it either. He didn't know why he'd had to turn back; he had his lifesaving badge and could swim fifty meters in twenty-five seconds, so he wasn't likely to drown. The only way to explain what happened is to say some great fear came over him. A better way might be to say nothing because I just don't know. Waves circled and sucked against the side of the boat. I felt my spreading bruise and pulled an incisor out of my bleeding gums, leaving a space where the dentist would later put a whiter tooth.

Johanna, who had stood to see the scene from the island, later, with her arm around me, told Andrew that she would never ride with him in a boat again. When he looked irritated, she said, "And Susan won't trust you again. I don't blame her."

Johanna, Andrew, and I camped in late summer hills. Andrew bragged that one day he would shoot a deer with an arrow. We could smoke the meat and eat just that and not have to lug things like Campbell's soup. And some day he might pierce his nose and wear a ring small enough so that it would not interfere with his lips.

At the top of the hill there was a pond where we decided to make camp. First we swam. When Johanna was kicking on her back, parting the algae with floating hair, three men came and sat by the pond. Andrew and I rose out of the water in our clothes arguing about who would get the dry towel. These men carried rifles and laughed when Andrew said he preferred arrows.

I didn't notice right away that Johanna was trapped by the men who were watching her swim. How did they know she wasn't wearing anything? Johanna was used to the world as she had made it for herself. These men sitting in the wet grass watching her didn't belong to it.

After an hour of treading water, waiting for them to go, she climbed out of the pond, ignoring the mud that sucked her in to the ankles. She walked her long naked body with its square shoulders into the woods and did not come back until they were gone. We knew that mood. She hoarded resentment. That night Johanna would not talk. For an hour or more she didn't answer me. Later, lying in Dad's World War II army bag, Johanna told us a story about a girl who'd watched her father commit suicide and then married a boring man and gone with him to Africa to do missionary work. Her hate for this man increased every day until the girl, with no life of her own, wanted to die. It was all in a book she'd read, she explained. I made her stop several times to ask questions. I could feel Andrew shuddering in the dark, not knowing how to deal with Johanna, whose mind did things he could, most of the time, keep his from doing.

Just as Johanna finished her story the men from some other county, the same men who'd interrupted Johanna's swim, walked toward the campfire. They stood before us with their guns. One of them grabbed Johanna, who put her head inside the sleeping bag as though it were a turtle's shell. Then the three men ran into the woods, one of them dragging Johanna folded inside the bag.

Andrew and I yelled for Johanna, but the men split up where the woods began, and neither of us could follow in the dark. The night was black. All the trees seemed like willow trees, dark fields of weeds hiding their trunks. The moon was behind clouds, and when the clouds moved, the campfire, which we built up until it became a bonfire, reached up toward the moon. Under the new light we stood around the fire howling like coyotes, pain softening our voices to sounds like singing. Then lower sounds like Buddhist chanting. We didn't know what to do.

In the woods by herself Johanna escaped from the man who had her locked inside the sleeping bag. The other two men searched for the third, the one who was supposedly carrying Johanna. When they found him, kneeling under a tree, Johanna was not with him. She had climbed up the tree. The men could not hoist themselves to the first branch. Their guns could have spread pellets through her belly. But no one wanted death; it wasn't like that. The men stood below with their half-bald heads and colored down jackets—one red, one orange, and one the color of a rabbit—looking up at her. She told me later she'd thought of spitting. She should have been spitting at them. But instead she drew her knees up and leaned against the trunk, supported on three sides by the branches near the treetop. In the morning, when Andrew and I found her, he looked at her and said, so that only I could hear, "In the olden days, she'd have been burned as a witch." I half caught her when she jumped down, and gave her a kiss. Andrew didn't.

And yet nothing that took place in Johanna's adolescence really changed her until the year Andrew began to date a maternal woman named Maggie, for it was during that year that Johanna's barn burned down.

Even the fierce men had not shaken her for more than a few days afterward; but perhaps the night in the tree marks the beginning of Johanna's understanding that feelings connect with experience and that, once you've had an emotion, especially an ugly one, there's no getting rid of it. When she was eighteen the barn turned to an acre of black hay. At the time, I may have blamed my father, because at breakfast he had often remarked that it was a "death trap" and an "eyesore." Really I blamed myself for not protecting it. That day, Johanna disappeared. Of course people whispered that she had burned with the barn. They spoke about it as if they knew. I watched people we knew come to see the fire die. And after it did, they stayed to find cat corpses and one cow corpse, but secretly they looked for her bones. Children collected what they thought were fingers. One claimed to have found the metacarpus bones. Someone else found a small clay container with several candies inside. Johanna liked to suck hard candies, I admitted, as though giving testimony. Another found a bottle of aspirin. There were several hundred singed beer cans.

I had not seen her roll up a sleeping bag, attach it to a pack, and kiss Mother and Father on both cheeks. My parents were concerned about college, and I was upset that she hadn't said good-bye to me. The day before my sister left Ontario, the day before the fire, we had shared a newspaper cone full of cashews. She told me everything that day, except that she was leaving. Then she told me that the barn was the best place for lovers, the only place for lovers, she had said, the only place for happiness. But then she had laughed suddenly and deeply. I didn't imagine it was the way she would someday cry.

My sister went traveling before I could give her any advice. I did not want her to wreck herself. What if she wasn't in the mood for hardship? I feared she'd be diminished by fending for herself in such a stubborn way, and I believe she was.

She went to the Yukon and became a waitress in a bar-restaurant in Dawson City. Though wages were high, the uniform, a long, old-fashioned dress with frills, included a bra that pushed up her breasts. The atmosphere brought back the time of the Gold Rush, and when the men called her "wench" it was considered fair.

With the money she saved she went to the mountains of South

America and raced as an independent on the skiing circuits in Chile and Peru. She wrote that there wasn't enough prize money. Europe was the place for professional skiers. What had happened to skiing only when she wanted to?

In Europe, Johanna joined a team of trick skiers. During the winter months the team traveled from resort to resort staging contests and daredevil shows. If I had known the right time and channel, I could have watched her on television. Sometimes the winners got their pictures in the newspaper.

Off-season, Johanna lived in Paris with an import-export man named Billy. When I went on a European concert tour sponsored by the Toronto Conservatory in November of the year I turned twenty-four, I visited them. I had not seen Johanna for three years.

Billy showed me his factory where he housed wild animals in order to sell them to rich people. Leopards, tigers, baboons went for high prices to North Americans bored with walking dogs and feeding fish. The other part of his business involved importing birds. He painted them secondary colors to make them look like exotic species from the rain forests. Then he sold them to collaborating pet shops in the U.S. and probably Canada too. Johanna didn't see what was so terrible about this as long as the birds were kept out of her sight.

She had changed. She walked quickly and wouldn't have noticed me in the window of a bus. She didn't see that Billy's hands had no hair and were smooth like caribou antlers, or that an old man's anger in the fruit store we walked by—"You bloody fucking son of a bitch," he'd screamed at no one in particular—meant something, or that hundreds of birds sitting in one tree is reason to stop and look. I could no longer imagine her saying she wished that cars would smash into one another while screeching to stop for a red light. We had talked about it when Johanna and I stood by some window, and I can't for the life of me remember the place or season. She didn't relish being leader the way she had, and her trim, athletic body, once so powerful, now struck me as small and neat.

Billy was six foot five and American. His French was decent, he told me, because he did business in French. His English was filled with regional clichés. When he first greeted me, he shook my hand, putting his free hand on my back, and said with feeling, "Howdy." After he showed me his factory, I didn't know what to make of him.

It was upsetting but not surprising to hear Johanna say her attraction to him was sexual, but when she first invited me over to have tea, which she still drank with cream and sugar, I couldn't hide my shock at what I saw. On every wall in the large, old, wood apartment there hung pictures of barns from all over the world. Photographs from New Brunswick of barns attached to houses in an L shape; lithographs and etchings of barns from Nova Scotia, Maine, and New Hampshire; barn paintings from Colorado, Alberta, and Kansas, "Where did you get them all?" I asked. Her European collection took up the four walls in the dining room. There were three large paintings of red barns from Australia and two black-and-white paintings of gray barns with stone foundations from New Zealand—North Island was printed on the matting at the bottom—in the bathroom. I could see how extraordinarily selective her collection was. "I bought them," she answered. The wood floors were left bare and unpolished. There was no room on any of the walls for Billy's trophies. Maybe he wanted to hang up a stuffed lion head. In his factory showroom he'd shown me the head of a tiger; its open mouth had been fashioned into an ashtray. "This is a hot item," he said, placing his hand bravely over its teeth. "It sells for ten grand."

Billy and Johanna attended my first recital in the small hall at the rear of a public library in the Marais section. Billy wore a tuxedo, which was inappropriate. Johanna held his arm, I noticed, and wore an elegant white knit dress. Her athletic walk and the aggressive bulge of her calves caused the dress to look funny on her, and I knew she'd be eager to get it off. I played Brahms, Schumann, and a little-known piece by Jean Sibelius. Afterward, Johanna told me I was a master. I explained that I was honestly more of a technician—the composers are the masters— which is the way I feel. She was effusive with her praise and made me think I'd made her happy. She invited me to stay with them the whole time I was in Paris. Billy took us to dinner at a place called Regine's that night, and during dessert they had an argument. Billy referred to Johanna in passing as "his loved one." She interrupted him and told him not to do that. He said, "Do what?" "Call me that," she said. "OK, I won't ever again," he responded in the angry voice of a ten year old. Then she called him petty. Johanna went to the ladies' room while Billy paid the check with a credit card. Alone with him, I told him I'd decided to stay in a hotel. I already had a reservation.

Billy called me up later in the week—I was scheduled to leave for Zurich in five days—to tell me Johanna was sick. I took a cab right over. She lay naked across the bed when I came in, and I saw on her buttocks a place where a doctor had taken skin to hide the result of some ski accident I hadn't heard about. We watched over my sister all night together, me on a director's chair, Billy standing. He took pictures of her while she dreamed of nothing and shadows scarred her elegant back. I don't know why I put up with the awful sound of the shutter clicking. He asked me if she'd cried hysterically as a child. "I could deal with it," he said, "if she told me why." I shook my head and glanced around at all the barns. When she vomited into my hands before dawn, Billy went to call a doctor. Alone with Johanna, I wanted her with that wild hair gripping her face gone from my life. I was beginning to have a life with my music, and I remember for a moment wanting her gone from it, because I had known her before, when she inspired me.

By the evening of the next day, she felt well enough to take vitamins and eat sherbet.

I came back two days later to talk Johanna into spending Christmas holidays with me and Andrew and our parents back at the farm. Billy told me she'd already gone with her group of skiers to break world records in events so dangerous they weren't in 1978 allowed into the Olympics. Some of the tricks she'd do were called things like double-daffy, spread-eagle, shoot-the-moon, Joan of Arc, man-breaker, barn-burner. Some didn't even yet have names.

A Leap of Faith

Dora tugged at the bedspread. Why could she never make it touch the floor on both sides? Her sisters didn't care anyway, she thought, as she picked up Iris and Delilah by their heads and set them back up against the pillow. There, she whispered. Peggy, her stupid roommate, was sound asleep. Do dress your dolls. She never answered anything about naked dolls and when they gave her stupid doll clothes for Iris and Delilah she threw them out the window. First feeling the large callous that was slowly eating up her foot, she then sprinkled powder into her sneakers and slipped them on, pressing closed the Velcro straps. Zip, rip, crackle. She made it work over and over again. Her knees were whole ever since she didn't have shoelaces tripping her: bad bows, not her fault. She remembered suddenly that last night she'd dreamed of roses. Peg had received them for her pneumonia and until Dora smelled the awful sweetness in her own room, right up inside her own head, it was what she'd wanted to name one of her sisters. Iris would have been Rose. But the names had been up to Dora's mother. Dora wasn't allowed to have children and so she had made Iris and Delilah her sisters. Everything had to be realistic.

She kissed Peg on the forehead because she didn't want her to die. Still, for being such a tattletale she deserved a punishment so before Dora left the room she pulled the petals off Peg's roses. She stared at them and not knowing what to do sat back down on her own bed and cried. Once she'd eaten a raw egg because someone forced her and she told that it was like eating a bad sneeze which had gotten laughs from her father a long time ago.

Poor Peg was moaning. Stop blubbering. Crying, I'm crying can't you see. Dora hated the word *blubbering* because she thought staff members used it to say there was no reason to cry when there always was and that made Dora want to scream. She scattered the petals onto Peg's Bible beside the vase where just the stems still stood in water so that Peg would think they'd fallen off by themselves and then quietly turned off the light and closed the door behind her. She smelled pancakes because it was Friday. The white ceiling in the stairwell closed around her and the idea of mother coming today. Mother coming, better than pancakes.

Dora looked down at her red plate. Danny on her right had a blue plate, and Bitsy, of course, tiny Bitsy way down at the end had green. The color of the plate told Sampson, the big woman in the white coat who served the food from a trolley, what size portion to put down. Dora knew it was somebody's idea to make them all think they were on a special diet, not just the FATSOS, the TUBS OF LARD. She was born hating to be called names— RETARD a long time ago—and now especially Door for short. Her stomach wanted more than one but her head told her no matter what the answer would be no and it was better to be friends with Sampson. She stuck her finger in her coffee to make sure it was hot enough for her rubber mouth. They called her "as-pest-os"—she could never say the word—"mouth." She slipped her arm around Sampson's waist. When Dora saw the older woman wiggle she let her go out of respect and then Sampson patted Dora's hand. It gave her goose bumps to be in good with staff.

"It's too muddy," Dora complained. She didn't like Dave to lead activity. She wanted Frank because he kidded better. Dave tried to make them sing songs at the same time as they walked around the pond. Frank let her sit down when she was tired, but not stupid Dave who told stories about Jesus Christ and his bleeding feet—"for you and you and you he died"—so today she faked a stone in her shoe. She never let anyone except the nurse see her feet because she knew what they did to lepers. There were ducks in the pond and she watched one waddle up onto the bank. Soft feathers on her lap. Did real people know how to make a duck cuddle? Dora's own mother okayed one big hug at the beginning. You're too old to cry and she would leave early. Pulling eggs down her throat. Today, Mother my friend.

A big machine that had a mind of its own with one long arm had spooned out the dirt to make the pond Dora remembered a long time ago and it still stood in her way. The big men with stomachs like Dora's who sat up high in the machine and some-times ate lunch in the restaurant where Dora waitressed were sourpusses, paying no attention to Dora not even to kid a little, pools of ketchup always left on their plates. Tomorrow at the hospital Dora was to be spooned out inside so she wouldn't bleed anymore. Her mother said she'd eaten peanuts at a party with the doctor who would operate. Dora herself had signed her whole name on a piece of paper. It had been up to her.

Baby pine trees had just been planted along one bank and other segments around the pond were roped off so you wouldn't accidentally walk over seeds trying to grow. Dora took a stick of sugarless gum from her pocket. Chewing, she looked beyond the duck playground, her playground too, and saw the bridge that connected the highway to the toll road that bypassed the city of Chicago. Sometimes groups including Dora went on the other road in a bus to the Museum of Science and Industry, never to Disneyland. Dora was always dimly aware of the sound of big trucks and buses and cars speeding by.

By eleven o'clock Dora was filling mustard bowls in the res-taurant. A man came in before the restaurant officially opened for lunch and it was Dora's idea that he be served anyway. Dora's supervisor, whom Dora had once heard someone compare to a chicken wing—for her toughness Dora understood—straightened Dora's apron with a tug, gave her a pad, and sent her out like having a small part in the Christmas pageant. Why did they never think she—Dora—could do anything?

The stranger was big like some of the workmen and he wanted salad bar, so Dora went with him while he filled his plate and explained what all the things were. Then she brought him Coke. Out the bay window where he sat in the curved booth she saw his huge truck where there was no parking allowed.

One bean at a time, she saw him eat, and knew she could beat him at cards. The last three times she'd gone out on her mother. Staff members liked to play cards with her too and Dora's mother said that somehow cards made Dora's brain work.

"I heard the pies were good here."

She didn't say: if she couldn't eat pie he shouldn't either. "Why don't you blink right?" she did ask, watching him put effort into each closing of his eyes. She poured him coffee. He didn't care her mother hadn't come.

Dora sort of knew Brenda was beside the kitchen door trying to get Dora's attention, always trying to boss Dora around, so Dora ignored her until Brenda came over and pulled her by the arm. "OK, OK," Dora said, bossing back in her way. By the time Dora returned to watch the man again he had already paid the cashier and gone. The shadow of his truck still loomed through the window. It was his coat she knew still hanging on a peg by the door. She found a pack of candy corn in the pocket and then hurried out to find him.

By then he was walking out the main road toward the toll-road bridge. Hiding under his hat, roped off; no hair. Dora felt her own thick hair, nice, except she still begged for permanents to curl it so more people would try to touch her head like her father had when he was alive. She sort of remembered Shirley Temple a long time ago. Standing on the walkway Dora heard Brenda's footsteps inside trying to find Dora. The man had reached the bridge and she watched him climb the stairs that ran up both sides allowing, Dora supposed, people to cross the big road. She'd never seen anyone go up before. Don't Brenda, that hurts.

Dora let the phone in her mother's house ring twenty-two times. Then she ate lunch in the kitchen off a plain white plate. She remembered who the man reminded her of. It was the man who made her bleed. When Dora was a girl she'd wandered off behind her house to where the railroad crossed a field and though she knew not to go on the tracks themselves—too scary anyway—when a man who was hidden back there like a spider she'd stared at in a gas station bathroom one day asked her to come sit on his knee she moved forward. Playing a game for a minute she ran away laughing. Tag, other children didn't let her play if she couldn't read or write. Without her underpants, young to have a beard down there, he said. No boils then. The next day she began to bleed and even though her mother told her that all women bleed Dora knew it was because he had touched her there.

Sirens sounded down the road and it just seemed to Dora that something was going on. Like a long time ago when she was a girl, she'd been left alone in the family house and found out her father had died of a heart attack on the tennis court where he had been winning five-love against a younger man. At the funeral everybody talked about all the details and she taught people how he had touched her—Dora—on the head. Nobody did it right. They brought him home wearing white and then suddenly changed him, black. Every weekend a long time ago her father took her with him to the hardware store where she got bored but always wanted to go again next time. Once after it seemed everything about her father was forgotten Dora screamed to her mother that she wished it had been her mother who died instead of him and her mother looked surprised and Dora knew that it was all more mixed up. Because she hadn't meant that, only that his legs had been so beautiful sticking out of white shoes. No, that her mother shouldn't yell at her. She'd tried to flush the KitKat wrapper down the toilet but it wouldn't go and Dora hated to be caught being too fat. It was on that day or the day before she'd agreed to her mother to have the operation.

Dora let the phone in her mother's house ring fifty times. Even Brenda felt sorry for her. Then Dora went out to see about the sirens. She saw policemen crawling inside the man's truck. Traffic stopped all along the road as far as she could see. There was a flashing light down under the bridge where the man had gone and done something wrong. Dora suddenly saw herself wearing a big hat in the Fourth of July parade. That was her on her dresser inside a silver frame. Maybe her mother had gotten stuck in one of the honking cars.

Dora dropped the man's coat when she figured out he had jumped a long way to be dead.

"He ate three pieces of pie," she told the policeman who was just watching and when he seemed excited by what she'd said Dora added, "They told me I could stop bleeding if I wanted."

Nothing was on television that night except the news and Dora and Peg never watched that. Peg had opened her eyes once. The nurse said Peg was still *very* sick and so Dora didn't hit her for snoring even though the noise disgusted her. She put her sneakers back on. Shaking her wooden board to hear the pins rattle she went out to the commons room to see if the house-mother would play cribbage. Not a day for mothers. Dora's had left only a message: Dora should be ready at 10:00 A.M. with a suitcase. Dora went to the front door and looked outside. Then she opened the door and—thinking of the way her mother tested a hot iron with a wet finger—spit into the darkness. Pain. She took a step feeling her stomach swirl like someone had flushed it. She'd never gone for a walk alone at night, never wanted to. In activity class last week they'd all gathered around Dora in a circle, the teacher and the rest of the class, and she'd been com-manded: Fall. They caught her and she had wanted to do it again but it was somebody else's turn. Leap of Faith the game was called. Not only Dora asked to play it again. They were never served Jell-O twice in a row.

Dora thought if you were on the outside like her mother and the truck man and all the people who had houses and babies you wouldn't want to play the falling game, but now as she began to walk toward the bridge with tears streaming down her big face she only knew the man asked her to follow him. There was nothing to laugh about this time. She couldn't see very well, the stones on the side of the black road, the teeth of a beast. She might trip and be swallowed. Dora walked slowly toward the bridge and though it had taken the man only minutes it took her almost half an hour to get to the stairs. She rolled the sleeves of her sweatshirt up thinking this might be how you catch pneumonia when you don't feel cold. Right foot, right foot, right foot. She forced herself up the stairs. Tears kept smoothing her face and she wanted to turn back but the man called her, his husky voice over her eyes, inside her ears. A naked man with bleeding feet had died for her too. Secretly she didn't believe that, only this.

When Dora made it to the top where the cars went by zip, zip, zip like turning a black-and-white television on and off she let go of the railing with one hand and wiped the tears from her face.

For now she knew. Now when she went back to the commons room and then to her own bedroom where she would pull the blinds, hug her sisters, and put her watch inside her jewelry box she would know why he had jumped waiting for the next day. And when she didn't like something she might think about what it was like up here on the bridge with the wind blowing about her like God was there. It would be horrible and she would try to laugh or shut her eyes up into a kaleidoscope but other times it would be like she could climb a mountain too if she wanted. Up here with the rubber-tire angels she learned a way to feel things to herself she could not explain.

My sisters wear no clothes. That man made me bleed. I know how to die, mother.

Callings

They came and went, filling her nights with such violence that she was almost glad her days now were uneventful. She guessed the nightmares had to do with her inability to face things properly. She went to sleep reluctantly, forced to please herself, for she'd either driven away or lost interest in every man she was ever involved with. (Women didn't like her that way or, it sometimes seemed now, any way at all.) She drank, but not so much, and counted her money, trekking out into the city's muddy snow once, sometimes twice, a day to review the numbers on the Citibank ATM. Three months ago, she'd lost her job. Her money supply, though still high by most standards, was less every week. She timed her tea bags now and saved them. White tulips in January—frivolous. She sold her silver and the pearls, which, anyway, were a symbol of the business job she'd once held. Her mother still loved her. "Come live with me," she'd offered. Never. Since losing her job, Anne knew she mustn't move too suddenly. Her imagination—in embryonic form—was trying to push its way forward. So far it worked to keep her from moving an inch: she felt committed to watching her own ruin.

Before business school, she had been likened to Diane Keaton, for Anne was tall and handsome and a bit scattered. But business had polished her, made her shine. She'd worked at her looks—exercise, facials, expensive clothes—with the intensity of someone whose job depended on appearances. But physical appearance was crucial in business only if you were trying to hide some inappropriate part of yourself, and, like most business executives, Anne felt she was. Giving off a sense of efficiency and of perpetual brightness counted more. This could be accomplished at Anne's company by a phrase here, a pungent joke there, a quick mathematical calculation, an overbearing remark, a neatly put-out report. All in all, that part had been easy for Anne to manage. And now her makeup wouldn't last forever, so she mostly stopped wearing it. She could handle sit-ups when she watched TV, but in three months without aerobic classes her underarms had gotten loose, and she lost her breath when being chased in her sleep. Who chased her? What was it she was so afraid of? She didn't know yet.

Hundreds had been let go, Anne's whole department banished for reasons to do with world economics, the future profits, and the directions of the Firm. The Firm. She'd called it hers, referred to "we" when the Firm made a move, a swerve. But this had been a swipe in her direction. She needn't have taken it personally. Lyle, Kate, Abel had all gotten other jobs. Headhunters still called her for her résumé, but Anne had lost it, left fifty copies at a sushi restaurant in a folder and never gone back. The disk it had been on hadn't been labeled, and now, anyhow, the disks with her work on them belonged to the Firm.

She clipped her toenails and spent a full five minutes looking for one that had been propelled under the couch. The cleaning woman whose husband had sometimes come just to watch her fold Anne's towels and underpants had been let go, and although Anne had gotten in the habit of leaving dry-cleaning plastic on the floor for the frail woman to pick up and red wine glued like a pool of dried blood in the bottom of deep hand-blown glasses, she now had to keep up with the dirt on her own, chasing toenails, fingernails wherever they flew. It felt good to be down on her belly, and when she found the thing, thick and clean like a shard of glass, she turned her head to the side, as if by staying still she herself wouldn't be heard or seen. For it had happened again, a noise from within her own apartment. It sounded human, like a sneeze or a high-pitched sigh. Please not now.

Full of dread for her brother, who, clearly, had again escaped from the halfway house and was in her closet, she fell asleep, there, under the couch.

She woke to the sound of birds bursting into song at repetitive intervals, and crawled out to answer the phone.

"So what are you doing?" the voice asked. It was Lyle, the man she'd worked with and slept with on and off for many years, calling from his new job. He'd been calling a lot lately. Last week he'd dropped by to borrow a cookbook.

"Sitting here in my terry cloth studying my toenail."

"Snap out of this. I've got an interview for you." Anne didn't answer. She was staring across at the Crozen painting she'd fallen in love with last winter. Over $10,000 it had cost her, and she'd bought it directly from the artist, so there had been no gallery markup.

"I'm hungry, Lyle. I haven't eaten since yesterday afternoon." She was still staring at the painting, which dominated the room entirely.

"Nine-thirty tomorrow at Drexel's offices."

"Shit, Lyle."

"The man's name is Bertrand, Philip Bertrand. You writing that down?"

"Yes," she lied, still occupied by the painting.

"OK."

"OK. Lyle. Thanks."

"OK. G'bye."

"Wait. You know that big painting in my living room?"

"I was at the dinner you gave for the artist himself. Remember?"

"It looks like it was painted with a gigantic piece of chocolate," she told him quietly.

"Eat something."

Lyle hung up, and Anne went over to the wall. She wiped her finger along the thickly smeared paint. Never had she felt so sure. She took the large unframed canvas down and turned its front so it faced the wall. Why hadn't she seen it before: the man couldn't paint. She ate imported tuna fish from the little glass bottle it came packed in (it had been around for so long she swallowed each bite suspiciously) and then bit into a red pepper as though it were an apple. She went to run the bath. A drop of oil made the water yellow and smell of juniper. She sat for several hours, replacing the water with hotter water when it cooled down. Anne hadn't really been fired like the others. She'd been told by her boss that hundreds were being let go, her whole department, but not her. She'd been called into one room and the people who were being fired into another. Afterward, she raced to her office to finish a report that wasn't due for three days. She was anxious to impress, to confirm her boss's decision to keep her. So she went to her secretary with sketches of diagrams she wanted her to add immediately to the report on the Wessel deal that was inside the Macintosh.

"I'm going to lunch first," the young woman answered.

"You're doing this first," Anne replied.

"Lunch first," the woman said, slinging her purse onto her shoulder.

"Absolutely not," Anne said.

"Fuck you. It's my right," she said back. As the girl stood to face Anne, shaking her many black braids, charmingly, defiantly, Anne's arm swung back, and to everyone's surprise—Anne's, the girl's, and the many witnesses'—Anne slapped her squarely across the cheek. The young woman screamed. It could have been worse, her dejected boss told Anne after firing her. At least prospective employers would think she'd been let go with the rest. They needn't know she'd struck a secretary, a black secretary who still might sue and win.

Had she hurt the girl? Anne wondered for the first time as her fingers, steeped in bathwater, puckered almost to the texture of walnuts.

❖   ❖   ❖

"Hope it was all right to let your brother in," the day operator said as he pulled open the heavy doors of the elevator. "He showed me pictures of you and him beside a Christmas tree."

"It's OK, Hank," she answered. "Harm's done." Anne smiled as she got in with him, realizing that she hadn't called Hank

"Lurch" in months. Lurch had been Lyle's nickname for him because of Hank's height and the ominous way he spoke and walked. Lyle had told her that when he was a kid he'd been obsessed with TV. He still told *Dick Van Dyke Show* jokes. Hank didn't seem to resent Anne for Lyle's poor wit. How could anyone resent her? He knew why she was always home now.

Outside, the wind swept back her scarf and lifted papers up from the sidewalk and then set them back down again. Damn, she'd been asked to bring a bottle of wine. There goes another ten dollars. Taxis went by her. Once she'd have raised her hand, let out a confident yell: Taxi! Out of the question now; even so, she wouldn't take the subways either. She'd not been down in seven years now.

Nothing wrong with walking to Lewis's. The Village to the Lower East Side would take her twenty minutes. The only reason she'd said she'd go to Lewis's had to do with sex. If she was honest with herself, she wouldn't mind a man right now, and with things the way they were, he might even turn out to be one that her mother would approve. Employment, money, status didn't impress her mother. Stuffed shirts. Bores. All she'd said about Lyle was, "He's got the dead eye, Anne, don't look at him." "How can I not look at him?" she'd asked. "I'm sleeping with him." "Don't look at him straight on," was her solution. "When you kiss him, keep your eyes closed." Well, she had had her eyes closed. Not just Lyle. All the men she'd gone with earned at least a quarter of a million a year, and—she wanted to face it now—that had impressed her. She'd actually believed there was a system working and the system allowed anyone who was smart and capable to make money.

Anne stood across from Astor Liquors, where she'd managed to find a decent wine for eight dollars. She was remembering headlines she'd read in the newsstand along her way. They were about the bear market and a bombing in Northern Ireland. It struck her that she hadn't read the paper in weeks, which would put her at a disadvantage at this particular dinner party. As she began to move again among the many people, she stepped into a puddle. It was then that a man dressed in layers of gray stopped her, or had she accidentally bumped him? Normally, she wouldn't have looked at him, not if she could help it. Unshaved, dark sunken eyes, lined skin. She didn't want to get close enough to smell him. Anne dug into her pocket and took out two coins.

"Bitch," he spat when he saw by the light of the pizza sign how much. He was right. The two nickels in her palm wouldn't buy the creamer for his coffee. She couldn't give him any more money because she didn't have much more with her. Instead she could ask him in. He would have to kick the mud off his shoes. Quickly, she became aware of herself again and saw where she was: in the middle of the sidewalk on a crowded street. The man looked at the package she held.

"Heads or tails," he said, taking one of the nickels and tossing it. He caught it and waited for her answer.

"Heads," Anne said, automatically.

"Give it over." With one hand the man showed her she had lost; the other he held out, waiting for his prize. What should she do? Anne hesitated and bought time by taking the bottle from the bag and reading the label. Hadn't she made her choice when she said heads? Anne gave the man the bottle with what turned out to be a polite amount of reluctance. Then he spat, not at her, just out of need, down at the ground.

"Heads or tails. Dry or sweet. You or me," he sang happily, sitting down on the curb to examine the bottle. After peeling off the seal, he raised the bottle in a salute. She saw that he was going to open the wine by smashing the neck against the curb.

"No. No," Anne objected. She caught his arm before he hit the glass against the cement.

"Fair and square," he pleaded, protecting the bottle by putting it between his knees. "It's mine."

"I'll just go and open it for you," she told him, amazed at her offer. Why was she doing this? She wouldn't be able to go to Lewis's now, not without the bottle of wine. She had touched his arm. She touched it again to reassure him. "I'll bring it right back, I promise."

Anne ran into the liquor store. It wasn't going to be easy getting someone to open it, Alcohol Beverage Commission regulations. As she went from one sales person to the next, she saw the man peering in the window at her, pressing his nose and lips against the glass, making a troll's face. Then he stood back and she thought he was smiling. The sales person at the last checkout counter sent her to the store manager. She explained to him that she had to taste the wine before deciding whether to buy several cases. He opened it for her. She sniffed the cork authoritatively, nodded, and told the manager she would think about the cases.

From outside, the man held the door open for her. He seemed to move with more bounce, and she noticed for the first time that he was wearing tennis shoes. Anne put the bottle forward, and he took it with both hands.

"Things belong to those who do best by them," he said confidently. But he had gone away from her. He had what he wanted. Anne repeated the catching sentence to herself.

"A touch woody," he said, imitating an upper-class voice as he moved yet further off. Anne laughed. Only after she'd walked on did she realize that she had nowhere to go now but back home.

She passed a row of young men selling odd-looking belts and dusty shoes, all of which were too small for her big feet. She looked with interest at first and then with relief: she could sell the Crozen.

Back in her apartment, she put on a nightgown and sat cross-legged on her bed. As she scanned her shelf for a book, she heard scratching noises inside the closet and then a loud, leisurely yawn. He must have heard her come in. Still, neither acknowledged the other's presence. Anne remembered well what happened the last time. She pictured breaking the news to her mother. The family, many years before when they were still a family, had decided to put Pete into a private institution, and her mother, now and again, appealed to Anne and Anne's father to reconsider the arrangement. Pete himself liked to remind them all that he deserved more than polite postcards—how about money, or records, or booze? he would write back. And then periodically he escaped.

Anne didn't feel ready to confront her brother. Without moving, without getting up to use the toilet, though she needed to, she fell back against her many pillows and slept close to the surface, her dreams mingling with her thoughts.

In the morning, seeing the closet door slightly ajar, Anne peered in. He had made a comfortable bed of the quilts and pillows stored there. She noticed crumbs around the closet floor, her shoes shoved helter-skelter to one side to make room, the pastel-colored mohair blanket in a heap, the size of the closet itself—large as any bathroom. She found the bottle she used to mist her plants and sprayed the cedar chips that sat in a little silver bowl on the shelf. This would bring out a lovely smell. Unable to think of anything else to do except wait for Pete to return, she changed into sweats, put her hair into what Lyle disapprovingly called the Pebbles Flintstone, a ponytail on top of her head, and forced herself to stretch, to do push-ups and a few leg-lifts. As she began remembering what happened the last time Pete showed up, her leg got too heavy to lift, and so she sat, pulling each foot onto the opposite thigh.

"Don't sting me," he'd pleaded. When Anne discovered Pete in her apartment sixteen months before, he was wearing one of her sheets over his head, shaking with fear that she was going to send him back to the clinic.

"Sting you?" She had to wash and change clothes and be uptown for a dinner meeting with prospective clients within an hour. She couldn't let Pete disrupt her schedule, and yet here he was, off his medication, off his rocker.

"But you're a rat. You'd rat on me."

"I don't even have time to think about whether I *should* rat on you." Anne flung off her shoes and ran into the bathroom to shower. She was under the water when he stuck his head in the door.

"You call these records?" he asked, holding a disk in at her.

"It works sort of like a cassette. Just stick it in the slot and tap."

Burning Spear was blasting as she toweled and dressed.

"La de da," Pete said with a whistle when she came out. He

looked her up and down. Anne pulled her sheer black stockings up underneath her dress and finished putting on makeup.

"Cost a lot, didn't it?" he said, feeling the arm of her black dress. "Probably more than a hundred dollars." Fortunately he didn't recognize cashmere and wasn't current on the price of style. "With your money you could buy elephants if you wanted to." She bent over to put on black suede shoes that made her his height and didn't notice Pete pick a safety pin off her dry-cleaning plastic. While she overturned a bottle of perfume against each wrist, he bent down and pricked her ankle.

"Bingo!" he yelled, watching her stocking split in two.

"God damn it, Pete." She ripped open another package of black sheer stockings, took off the pair he'd ruined, and threw them at him. Pete rolled up his sleeves and drew the stocking legs over his arms. He began prancing around the room in time to the music.

"I'll be the helicopter," he said. Running out of the bedroom, he twirled the length of the living room, his black arms held more like an insect's antennae than like fuel-propelled blades. A glass jar overturned. Anne remembered: when they were kids he always played the noisy parts—the guns, bombers, and helicopters—in neighborhood war games. Pete had had so many friends. Some days after school he and his army took over the kitchen. They ate chocolate milkshakes with spoons from large mixing bowls. Pete always offered Anne bites. He was voted president of his junior class. The same year he built a darkroom and photographed blades of grass, a girl frowning behind a chain-link fence. Anne remembered one he'd taken of her. She'd felt flattered until, in the developing of it, he'd purposely distorted her face. Maybe that was how she looked to him now: convex.

"The neighbors," Anne said, as she turned down the reggae music. She was nearly ready to go. Pete still waved black arms and had since put the seat of the panty hose over his head. He turned his dancing into fencing steps, and Anne stopped to watch the familiar movements he aimed at the living room lamp, thrusting and backing off. They'd practiced the sport together as teenagers; it had been their father's sport. Once there had been talk of Pete being Olympic fencing material. At about the same time, Anne got involved for a few months with a peace activist. They'd had sex in East Rock Park. She remembered how she'd used her new sophistication to get Pete to quit the sport. Pete kept the fencing pantomime going.

"Don't break anything," she said, as she went back to get her purse and shawl. She couldn't think of what would interest him. If she'd been able to, she might not have been so afraid to ask him the things she knew she was supposed to ask. Where's your medication? Should I call the clinic? Do you need help?

When he saw her standing all ready to go, her purse slung over her shoulder, her hair hitting against her long neck at a sharp, confident angle, her lips red, her face shiny and smooth from lotions, he maneuvered into the kitchen and came out to face her, fencing still, with a large kitchen knife.

"Where's your foreign accent?" he asked.

"Accent?" Anne sniffed her wrist. It was the name of her perfume.

"You look like a whore," he said, dancing forward, elegantly.

"I can't dodge you in heels," Anne responded, noting that, despite his grace, he'd gotten a little fat. She saw it only when he had his head covered. His face, more babyish now than when he was younger, was still appealing. She wished he would let her see it. As a teenager, the range of expressions he commanded had made him seem handsome. "It's not fair," she said, dodging as best she could.

"It's not fair," he imitated in a high girly voice.

"You used to like the way I looked."

"Cathy doesn't wear makeup." Pete hovered toward Anne with a lunge and then retreated neatly.

"Cathy?" she asked, putting down her purse. Quickly she glanced at the door, but he saw her.

"She was the only girl I've seen in the last three years that I wanted to go out with. She had these straight white teeth." Pete bucked his own teeth to show Anne. "She caught me staring at her mouth."

"Yeah," Anne said, aware that he had forced her to pay attention to him.

"It's like the girl has to be as sick or sicker than I am or I'm not even allowed to try for her."

"Who told you that? You can try for anything you like."

"Like you," he said, the knife aimed at her belly.

"Please, Pete, don't."

"I'm scaring you, aren't I, and I didn't even mean to."

"At least take off the stockings. Then we could talk."

"But you've got a date."

"It's a business meeting, I told you."

"So why are you dressed like that?"

"I don't know," she said. Had he heard something honest in her voice at last? He put down the knife.

"I need some bucks," he said, as he drew the stockings off his arms. He'd worked up a sweat from his fencing, and to Anne the wet smell mixed into the sheer nylons was repulsive. Anne knew she shouldn't give him money. She had to go. She took out fifty dollars and handed it to him. When he had it in his hands, he began walking around the living room on his toes, wiggling his behind in imitation of her on high heels. She opened the door and looked back at him.

"I've got rights, too, you know," he said, looking up at her. He sat on the floor, flung his thick hair off his face, and dealt the money out into neat rows as though each bill were a card and the family had gathered around to play a game of concentration. He took off his shoes. She closed the door.

Anne's face got hot, remembering what happened next. God, she'd stayed away that night. Left Pete on his own. And she'd gone home with one of the men she'd had dinner with—OK, not just any man, she'd had her eye on him for some time—and returned to her apartment early the next morning to change for work.

Pete was asleep on the floor fully dressed. There was a strange older man, a street man from the looks, beside him. He was also fully dressed and sound asleep. Three empty liquor bottles sat on different surfaces, a fourth tipped over onto her expensive rug, bought on a trip to Arizona. The stain, she could tell, was permanent. The power light was lit on her stereo, disks strewn around it. The video machine sent off a deep fuzz.

She picked up several of the videotapes to see what they'd been watching but knew beforehand. Anne glanced at a piece of a sweet roll they had left on a paper bag and went into the bathroom to extract her diaphragm. Then, she called Lyle and explained the situation. How could she have known that he'd bring the police? Hearing about the porno flicks had offended him. She'd never understood Lyle's attitude toward sex. He went endlessly out of the way to create the perfect moment, only to be thwarted by something he hadn't considered like a little gas in his stomach or a salty taste on Anne's skin. She'd gotten used to having other lovers. While the policemen threw her brother up against the wall, handcuffed him, and dragged him away—and all through it Pete coughing and vomiting—Lyle cornered Anne in the kitchen. She'd tried to get away to help her brother, hadn't she? But she was crying too hard to give Lyle much of a struggle. He wouldn't relent. He wanted to know where she had spent the night.

❖   ❖   ❖

The phone rang, and Anne released herself from the almost lotus position to answer. Pulling herself back into the present, she wondered: why had she sold Pete out that day?

"Asshole," the voice on the other end said. It was Lyle.

As if he didn't have one himself, she thought, as if it were at once the most imaginative and cutting thing he could say to her. Asshole, Anne knew, could also be a temporary insult. A good friend could be one as well as an enemy. She waited to see which meaning she'd been dealt.

"You didn't turn up?"

"I don't want that job, Lyle."

"Listen. It wasn't so bad what you did. A lot of people wanted to hit Angel."

"I didn't *want* to hit her. I just couldn't help myself."

"So what are you going to do?"

"You keep asking me that." She pictured him in his office, the haughty shape of his silk tie bulging at his throat and, directly above it, his chin in two distinct lumps, soft and clean. She saw his immaculate hands, one resting on the slick wood surface, the other working the telephone as if with its DID and ISDN capabilities it was as much a part of him as his tongue or his curly blond hair.

"You could have at least called the guy and canceled. Bertrand would have taken you. I happen to know he thought you were dynamite."

"Sorry, I didn't think of it. I've been sitting here thinking about something else." Anne paused as though losing her way. Then she jumped back in, loudly: "What did you tell the police that time when they came to get Pete?"

"What?" he asked, incredulous.

"What did you tell the police to make them beat Pete up that way?"

"Can you hold? My secretary wants me." She pictured his finger teasing over the switch hook.

"You put me on hold and I'm gone," she said.

"Where do you get off? You've been fired," Lyle gave a little laugh (it was his "I'm partly impressed" laugh), "and you act like a fucking star."

"I'm done, Lyle," she said flatly.

"What's his name?"

"I wish there were someone."

"I've been thinking. Remember I told you I'd give you mother's ring?"

Anne sat up and held in a laugh. She'd never seen Lyle so desperate.

"Things belong to those who do best by them," she answered and then laughed good-naturedly.

"Where did you get that line? Since when did you become a Socialist? Miss businesswoman. Miss corporate finance. You don't even know who's on top in Cambodia. What's the capital of Ethiopia? Come on."

"Lay off, Lyle."

"You've met some liberal literary creep."

"There's no one," Anne answered quietly.

"Let's just forget we had this conversation. I've been so uptight lately. They've got me doing artificial intelligence for insurance companies."

"They promised you finance," she said. She was surprised Lyle had let himself get cornered like that.

"Friends?" he asked in a voice that was deep and even. It was easy to love his voice.

"Asshole," she reminded him.

"OK, so feel sorry for me. I'm looking out at Radio City Music Hall and the profile of St. Paul's."

The same view every day, Anne thought. The same person every day: handsome, educated, privileged, white. Anne got up from the couch to look at the clock on the church steeple out her east window. The receiver fell under the coffee table and hit the floor hard.

"You put me on hold," he was screaming when she came back.

"I don't have a hold," Anne answered.

"Then you just walked away, which is rude."

"Listen Lyle," she began, but he saw what was coming.

She didn't interrupt him when he said he had to go because his secretary was calling him. He would tell his friends that he'd been the one to break it off. She'd gotten too weird.

Anne knew what she wanted to do. She sat, her legs stretched out, her head back against a pillow, and planned out every detail. What color paint she would use and where to buy it. She'd bring the can back up to her apartment and refuse to tell the doorman what she was up to. No one must know. Even Pete would think she'd gone mad. He would hold his breath as she dipped the brush in and made the first broad stroke. But she didn't want

Pete to see, not until it was finished. She'd continue to slop the paint over the canvas to cover the brown smears. When it was done, gleaming clear and white—a blank space—and she had given it time to dry, she'd pull the cover off the top of a marker and write in gigantic letters: WELCOME PETE.

She could still see herself, though faintly now, walking the halls of the Firm, bending to take some water from a fountain beside a large plant, rising, lips wet, turning into the main conference room. She always knew beforehand what she would say in meetings. Herself: leaning back into the plush chair in the padded room, flicking the heel of her foot in and out of its pump. A man—they were almost all men in the conference room that day, men heading for forty or fifty—made a point and illustrated it by drawing three intersecting circles onto the framed marker board. Anne sat forward to make a counterpoint and was listened to, though her voice sounded more feminine than was strictly right. She'd been sent to a class to learn how to give speeches. After reviewing a videotape of herself speaking, her instructor told her to lower her voice, be more forceful. She winced remembering how her hips had swung. No one dared say out loud, don't swing your hips, but it had been there for her to see. Anne stood and swaggered into the kitchen, enjoying her own exaggeration of her walk. The floor needed sweeping.

She bent to pick up a penny that had fallen and went back to the couch. Of course she couldn't really touch the painting. It was a question of rights. She'd never even dared what Crozen had. Anne ate a piece of bread cut from a Balducci's loaf—she'd gotten used to its fine quality and hadn't given the store up entirely—then found a blank piece of paper. She walked over to her desk, sat, and wrote what she'd dreamed of writing in bold letters across the canvas. But now she wrote in her small neat script on ordinary paper and put the note inside the place her brother had made his own.

The Retreat

Not one of the four large-breasted, narrow-hipped young girls saw their mother put on her hiking boots and the dowdy Chinese coat that looked like a quilt and begin her trek up the mountain. If they didn't already sense it was time for her retreat, then her absence would soon remind them. Cheese, bread, fruit, milk, wood for the stove. It was there for them. She'd conceived them all while in love. The death of her son had poisoned that love, and she'd pushed the father away from the community where they all lived. She stoned him down one afternoon while he was eating corn chips in the hammock behind the house he'd built with skylights and a deck. In doing so she had broken her vow of peace. With his heavy beard and black chest hair creeping onto his back, she'd had no trouble pretending he was a dog.

In one hour she could climb the mountain behind the pond, up the steep path she and her friend Sharifa remade every year by swinging at the brush with scythes. They'd marked the path by painting blue moons on the gray tree trunks, then placed clusters of rocks at intervals to tell the others how much further to go. She was sure that no one who lived in the community consisting of twenty-four privately owned houses, each on a six-acre lot, knew what she'd done to her husband to make him go away. The stoning took place ten years ago, and ever since her face to the world had been serene. Who could have guessed she was capable of such violence?

As she headed toward the pond across the road from her house, she hoped her daughters might hear the noise of her boots in the muddy grass and begin missing her. The view of the pond, even in its winter condition, aroused memories: she thought of the snapshot of her daughters, at fourteen, fifteen, sixteen, and seventeen, floating in their inner-tube boats, drinking artificially sweetened lemonade through straws. They all wore dark glasses and one-piece black bathing suits. These they had declared the summer's fashion. Large boys—hunks, Sharifa called them—swam around her girls like sharks.

She didn't push her spiritual world upon her daughters and in fact encouraged them to look away. She kept her religion veiled. The meditation room on the third floor was off-limits to them. They didn't help her hang up the omens, nor did they learn the Sanskrit chants, or attend the early morning ceremonies she presided over. She once came upon one of them torturing a frog, and turned away. Still, they saw the respect with which others treated their mother's words; for themselves, they felt her power mostly in her silences, her poise. She often told them stories instead of scolding them and was able to laugh when any of her children was clever enough to turn a story to her own advantage.

They didn't know about the stoning of their father. After he'd left, she continued her job running the rape clinic in town. Her house was paid for, and money from the man who'd hit her son with his black BMW filled her savings account. She began eating chicken and beef again and also started raising peacocks. Now, several of the males were mature, and she could make them display their fans at will; they responded to the booming sound of her voice.

She crossed over the sandy beach where nude sunbathing was in one year, banned the next, and entered the forest above. After a hundred yards or so, she stopped in front of a mound, lit the candles in colored glass jars surrounding it, and then, with her hands raised to the sky, knelt down suddenly, as though struck on the back with a board. She didn't cry anymore. Sometimes, like now, she let out a long, deep scream. It was here, on this inconspicuous spot, without even a view of the pond, that she had buried her seven-year-old son. The community, her husband, and her four baby girls stood around her on the terrible day, stunned by what had happened, but, like always, she took the reins. She chose the spot in defiance of civil law and presided over the funeral, fed everyone at her home afterward, and played the flute while they sang the notes that were written on sheets of music she'd gone to town to photocopy earlier in the day. She slept on the floor that night because, even with all her wisdom, she blamed her husband, his male energy, for the death of her child.

"You and your machines," she said to him. He was so hurt, he'd been unable to look beyond her cruelty and so fed it.

She screamed once more, loudly, letting the sound come out of her until she was out of breath, then stood and looked around, aware that she'd aroused small animals and birds, unseen, around her. She found the path again and headed upward. Two days of silence, exercise, meditation, fasting. It would do her good, enable her to focus on whatever was keeping her spirit from moving ahead. She took a rest at the one-mile mark and heard the call of her oldest peacock, Peter. She understood his harsh wail. Like her own, it signified loss.

Only a month ago, she'd woken up one morning aware that some disaster had occurred while she and her daughters slept. When she went out to get wood, she found Peter's mate, Jezebel, lying limp on the walk. The bird had fallen from the second-story porch after her neck had been severed almost in two. Insects dove into the gouge on the neck of the big brown bird, and the other birds, some of them Jezebel's babies, hopped around her plain body. When the same thing happened to a second bird the next night, she took the body to a neighbor who said he thought the murderer was a panther. When she lost a third bird on the following night, in precisely the same way, she grew desperate. She didn't believe in guns—neither in hunting nor in war—and could not justify an exception. She came up with a plan. With the poker beside her and the door to the porch open so that she could hear the slightest noise, she went to bed afraid only of her own strength. She would kill the killer.

Several hours later she heard a gentle flutter, a disturbance in the air as slight as a person swallowing, and crept along the hallway, holding the poker like a sword. She wore no clothes at all. Taking the two steps to the porch in a hunched position, she saw her birds where they slept, and then suddenly, from nowhere, something came down from the sky and was on top of Peter's back, going straight, she felt, for his wondrous fan. Dropping the poker, she lunged at whatever it was. When she had her arms around the thing, trying to match her strength with its own, she felt that she would win by squeezing. A physical strength unlike any she'd felt before came to her. She didn't doubt that she could kill the thing with her bare hands. For assurance, she went for the poker. Still holding onto the animal—what on earth was it?—she quickly grabbed the weapon. It was then that one of her girls, Lisel, turned on the lights. Just as the porch flooded with brilliance, the animal struck her on the hand. The pain made her let go of it, and she stepped back and made a warrior's movement forward as though to stab the creature. But now, in the light, she could see what it was, a great horned owl. The squat bird was more dazed than she by the light. She could kill it with a stroke.

But then she heard, in the same instant the desire to kill it took hold of her, a small sound escape her daughter's throat. The sweetness of the sound brought her to herself. She dropped the poker on the stone floor, filling the porch with a cruel metal ring. Then she grabbed the stunned owl and turned it upside down. Suddenly the bird was completely tranquil. It hardly seemed to breathe. She and Lisel stored the bird in an empty garbage bin. By then her other daughters were awake, kissing their mother for her heroism.

"How did you know to turn it upside down?" Lisel asked.

"It came to me," she answered.

"How?" Hera wanted to know.

"Divine inspiration," she said, smiling. She noted the quizzical looks on her daughters' faces. Before one of them could say something common, like "Give me a break, Mom," she went quickly inside.

"It could have killed you," the warden of the Virginia Wildlife Preserve told her the next day. By then the slit on her hand where the owl had only just nicked her with his talon was pulsing and swollen, her entire left limb useless. She wore it in a sling.

"What will you do with the owl?" she asked the warden. Killer though it was, she was now worried about what would happen to it.

"Send it to a training school for birds where it will learn how to kill pests, mostly mice," said the warden. "Once it's trained, we'll let it go."

She could see Hera's rock now against the gray sky. When her middle daughter was approaching puberty several years before, she'd declared the rock her own, and everyone in the community had respected the claim. Two spots of green lichen sparkled on its immense surface, looking to her like eyes in a face, a great round rock face: her own. It wouldn't be long to the top now. She took mittens from up her sleeves and smiled at the woolen strings with which she'd attached them to her coat. She was as bad as her daughters about losing things. At the place where the path veered around Hera's rock, she stepped aside and began to climb up it. At the top she could see down, beyond the pond, beyond the house, the community, the countryside, the town, into the horizon, which looked, suddenly, not far away, but close. So close upon her was the landscape that she couldn't for a moment distinguish a single feature. Usually, she'd have a profound moment in front of such a sight, something would trip in her brain, she would have her thought, and then, afterward, for a brief, guilty moment she would allow herself to acknowledge her own gifts. But this time when nothing came her body shook as though to a rock-and-roll fragment. She felt small and insignificant suddenly, even though she was a big, proud-looking woman. Then she remembered that to her girls she was a source of authority, wisdom, and, probably, good. Still, as she looked down and took a breath of the cool winter air, both musty and pungent like the taste of purple sage, all that came to her was a child's song: "I'm the king of the castle and you're the dirty rascal." She sang the ditty out loud and then jumped down.

With lightness unbefitting her forty-eight years, she ran to the little house that served as a retreat for the entire community. She undid the string that fastened the door and entered. The small, dank room, even in the cold darkness, felt like a shrine. She lit one candle, then the others. Once she had the wood burning furiously in the small, rusted stove, she sat back on the mattress, piled high with folded blankets and a nylon sleeping bag, and put her feet on the worn Turkish rug. The smell of incense was so strong, she realized somebody must have been here recently. It was that smell, cinnamon-like and churchy, that brought her back to her purpose. She was here to meditate and fast but also to write. She looked at the stack of writing books under the window and took the top one down. Before writing in the books, she always read the newest entries, moving backward until she got to her own last entry from several months before. She opened the book and paged forward to the last entry. Odd. No one had signed it. Without reading, she closed the book. She got herself undressed and into the blue bag, shaped like a mummy, and slept.

Silence woke her. She lay still for hours blinking, hungry. Only when the light came directly into the room, only when a beam of sunlight hit her face, could she move. After dressing, she saluted the sun, her body bending perfectly with each pose. All through the series of movements, she was aware of the book and, when she'd finished, went over to it and put her hand on top. Before she could stop herself, she took it back to the bed, opened it up on her lap, and read:

> When I was a child, I saw my mother take a bucketful of stones, like they were tennis balls and she was going to practice her serve, and throw them at my father. Somehow, he managed to back into his car and drive away. When he was gone, she finished throwing the stones that were in the bucket and began

picking others up from the driveway. She was still throwing
them when I snuck away.

Who would believe it? It had been just as Hera—it was Hera's
handwriting—described it. She read this account of her actions
again and afterward looked at the top of the page, dated only
one day before. She grabbed the page as though to tear it out, but
stopped herself. There was another way. She dug her teeth deep
into the pencil.

She could tell her daughters what they already knew, how,
many years before, her husband had attached a motor to her
son's skateboard. Before her son had mastered the toy, he sailed
out of the community's private road onto Route 50 where the
cars went by at high speeds. She found him lying on the front
seat of the black BMW that had hit him, dead but intact. The
driver, in suit and tie, was bent over on his knees, crying with his
face touching the hot tar road. She could explain how she'd
blamed not one man but two. Not only the driver, who later
offered her money—kept pushing money on her with as much
energy as it had taken him to make it—but also the man who
had attached a motor to a toy. As far as she was concerned, his
time had come: her husband had to go.

She shook her head. She couldn't argue that anyone might
have done as she had done given the circumstances. Or that she
was no longer the same person. Only a child makes excuses.
Where was her art? What she finally wrote gave her more pain
than anything she had ever said or done:

> Whether you are sinless or not, cast your stones at me. I enjoin
> you. I am just a mother who has lost a child.

It took her a minute to know she was finished writing.

When she was sure, she stood. Her aura overwhelmed the
small room. She picked up the ax hanging on the back of the
door, meaning to spend some part of the day chopping wood.
Soon there would be other visitors, and she wanted them to be
warm. Hera would tell her sisters what their mother had written;

they would defend her. Alas, that was perhaps her punishment, to continue on as before. She tried, as an exercise, to make the small flute sound that had come from her daughter's throat. Embarrassed by the unlikely noise, she bent toward the book and turned the thick page back to her own entry. She signed by wetting her dirty thumb with her tongue and pressing it to the page.

A House Guest

"'She can do everything *and* she's beautiful,' that's what Jacqueline said about you."

There was no response as she swung closed with one hand the black-spotted chintz curtains she had made. His wife held their two-year-old girl in her other arm. Gordon, seated on the edge of their queen-size bed, thumped his upper body down on the cover that matched the curtains, loosened his tie, covered his eyes with one huge arm, and crossed the other over his forehead for protection. She was coming toward him. As his wife brought her fist down hard on his chest, Gordon groaned loudly. He heard her leave the room to put Anna, who was glued with saliva to a stuffed ostrich, to bed.

"I'll be back," Tina yelled as though she'd seen him peeking.

Under their own tribal code, devised over ten years of living together, he recognized that he'd asked for it.

"Oww-whoo," he howled: part wolf, part dog. If she thought it hadn't hurt, she might do it again.

Tina returned in a white nightie, her fake gold Egyptian beads still around her neck. He re-covered his eyes with just his hands. He couldn't hit her back, but he could call her anything he wanted, and the pain in his chest had brought forth a beauty. Furthermore, if the argument got really bad he could always sleep in the garage on the leather seats of his car with the doors locked against this—he wasn't ready to try it out yet—She-Bitch-From-Hell. He considered using his "oh save me" routine, where he pretended the bed was a raft on the ocean and he was falling off it, but decided that act worked only when sex was at least a remote possibility.

"How do you think this makes me feel?" she asked, and the way she asked it, emphasizing the word *feel*, putting her hand on her chest where it touched his favorite bone, the one that stood out below her long neck like an ivory mantelpiece, reminded him that the phrase and the hand gesture went together. Did she think she was in a soap opera? At any other time, with her great mother's breasts he had loved from every possible angle swaying out of his reach before her, as if she were on her knees making them move like that on purpose, dazzling new pink still on her lips, her beauty would have inspired him to clown. He laughed out loud thinking of what Alex Katz or, better yet, a great artist like de Kooning would do to her. He and de Kooning were now one: She-Bitch-From-Hell.

"Must you speak in clichés," he said. He moved this pawn forward confidently, aware that "How do you think this makes me *feel?*" counted as a cliché only because of the way she'd exaggerated the word *feel*. Psychobabble. It occurred to him that he could lie about Jacqueline. "It happened only occasionally," he could say, or, closer to his truth, "She made me." He pictured himself saying with more flip sophistication than he knew he could get away with, "Jacqueline was into S and M, what can I say?" But Gordon couldn't even remember if anyone used the term *S and M* in 1970. The only reason Tina would believe, more or less, any accusation he might make was because he had a long-established record of truthfulness. Gordon figured a lot of people would be surprised—all those clients for instance who thought of him as an overly aggressive businessman—to learn he didn't generally tell lies, especially ones that would enable him to avoid conflict with his wife.

Gordon put his hands through his hair, combing it back Edwardian style the way Tina had fixed it for him at the start of the evening. He sat up and looked the effect over in the mirror that hung between the two fabric-covered windows. Slapping the sides of his once-handsome face (recently it had gotten a little fat) he thought about how, when he was younger, the sight of his innocent looks had made adversaries want to hit him. No, he wouldn't start lying now. He smiled up at himself and then over at Tina. He didn't mind a bit of trouble.

"You see, you don't even deny it," she said.

"Listen to me Tina," Gordon said, effecting a tired voice. Although Tina didn't know it, they were really arguing about something that had happened fifteen years ago. "Try to imagine Jacqueline's motives."

"You think she's still in love with you?" He felt tremors of skepticism beneath her question.

Was it so impossible? he wanted to ask.

Sometimes he felt he couldn't say what he honestly thought to Tina anymore. Thoughts like, for instance, that maybe—only maybe—he didn't want his daughter to attend the neighborhood preschool. Tina would call him a racist. When he woke up last Sunday in the country where they'd gone for a romantic weekend and began talking about wringing the neck of a shrill bird, she'd called him a species-ist. Could she really have been talking about animal rights? Soon his own daughter would begin sneering at him for crushing slow flies with a paper-towel wad and then flipping them—two points—into the waste basket. Now he felt almost sorry; this woman for whom all forms of humanitarianism were sacred had a husband she suddenly imagined was a rapist or at the very least a rapist sympathizer.

"What I think," he said, "is that Jacqueline can't help seeking revenge for any pip-squeak hurt any man—and there have been lots since I ducked out—might have caused her—including me."

"But she's not the one you were fighting with," Tina said. And, clutching herself as though she were cold, she emphasized her point, "It was *me*, you and me who were fighting."

"Who kept bringing up the subject? Think about that for a minute. She brought up rape four times. Four times," he held up the fingers of one hand, "during the course of one dinner party. Do you know why?"

Tina said nothing.

"Because she loves to sit back and watch us fight. It's like flicking on the TV. She knows the name of the show and the right channel. And to think we got her invited to that party."

"Shh, she'll hear you."

"I hope she does hear," he said, his hands up around his mouth megaphoning his voice upward to the third-floor guest room where Jacqueline, whom Gordon had known well ever since they'd been in almost all of the same art and literature classes at the small liberal arts college where they'd met, was spending the night.

"And why would she want to egg you on?" Tina stood up. He watched her grow to her great height that normally made him proud.

"We had a complex relationship." Gingerly, he brought the queen out from the back row.

"But we were fighting about the woman in what's-her-name's legal case—the woman with the birthmark."

"And the pink stiletto shoes," he added.

"That's prejudicial," Tina objected. "Like calling the victim a hooker."

"Pink high-heeled shoes then," he said in an apologetic voice. Again, he put his hands over his eyes. "The rape case that ditsy lawyer was telling us about was the conversation on the surface. When Jacqueline's in the room, there's always a subtext: her health or feminism or Zionism or the problems of the rich. And if the subtext were properly footnoted aloud it would scream: me, me, me, me, me."

Wondering whether or not he was safe, Gordon took his hands away from his eyes and looked over at his wife. Although Tina knew he had been involved with Jacqueline, Jackie as she was called back then, he couldn't explain about the kind of sex they'd had.

Jackie was different from other women. A third gender (could it be true?) to which more and more women were converting. He tried to reel it back, back to the days when higher education really was opening up and his scholarship had paid for everything—college tuition, meals, his bed, his sheets. The big challenges consisted of reading stacks of books, building post-Bauhaus architectural models, seducing women, and earning enough money to pay for records. If you were spiritually minded you took your girlfriend (or she took you) to the woods. Otherwise, in your room (Gordon had put his mattress on the floor and stretched planks across wooden blocks to stack his books on) candles substituted for the moon. Gordon owned one of the smallest record collections at the college. Jackie, he remembered, never put them back in their jackets. He remembered too the thump, thump, thump of the needle as he fell asleep. The thumping kept Jackie awake all night, but she wouldn't get up to stop it. At breakfast she declared that she was an insomniac and added that she sometimes spent all night wandering the aisles in the A&P. She was unfaithful, or was it that the concept of fidelity didn't then exist? There had been something about her ovaries causing her pain, and during those days she also talked some about killing herself. Jackie's face: full of freckles, as though each one—she once told him this—stood for a lie she'd told or something bad she'd done. Her face: teasing, awake, twisted, cute; her nose, uplifted like her breasts, sniffing for attention; her fingers blunt and tricky, he knew, remembering the first time she'd put one of them up inside, surprising him. If you didn't surprise her back, the life went out of her face. For a long time he wanted to tell her to make her tongue more secretive; he didn't because he knew how much she hated criticism.

She'd grown up with the kind of facts college tests reward you for, and her memory—uncluttered with the baseball and basketball lore that filled Gordon's—worked better than his. She was more coordinated than he—though he could run faster—and her wit—that's what irked him the most—wasn't the least bit feminine. Sometimes she even beat him at chess. Competitors more than lovers. Now Jackie pretended to be grown up and had managed during visits over the years to become one of his wife's best friends. Tina and Jackie wrote letters and chatted on the phone. One year he and Tina received an expensively printed Christmas card with a photograph of Jackie and two men (boyfriends?) unzipping their wet suits. Gordon had pointed out that only someone very rich would have the nerve to do that. And yet somehow his wife continued to see the small, capable, shrewd sort of woman that Jacqueline—at thirty-seven—pretended to be. Tina wanted to make Jackie Anna's godmother. Now there was something they should be fighting about.

"Jacqueline's mind is like a wine cellar," he told Tina, trying another angle. "She stores as many facts as she can, and years later they come out altered, improved on. She makes facts— headaches can signal a brain tumor—into stories—the doctor at Mount Sinai told me I cured my own brain tumor."

"At least *you* tend to tell the truth—that's something."

Gordon wanted to tell her she was missing the point. Sure, he told the truth, but it was for the same reason that Jackie exaggerated it. It was conflict they both went after, and for Gordon truth could almost always lead you there.

Gordon saw things differently now that he worked twelve hours a day and was nowhere near as successful as he'd once assumed he'd be. As a man who ran his own business so tightly that he couldn't afford to get sick, he didn't like to remember that he'd picked his college because it had a high woman-to-man ratio. And at a time when the guys he'd gone to high school with were either pounding nails or dying. That was hard enough to understand. There had always been books beside his bed—Aristotle and García Márquez and T. S. Eliot. Jackie knocking on his door and right away poking her head in. Every moment had to be inspired. Most of the students knew from the beginning that Jackie, the mouthy girl with the short red hair and green eyes, had millions of dollars, but she'd won respect by pretending to be just a student too. She didn't throw her money around. Gordon wondered, as he sat there on the bed in the wake of his failed explanation to Tina, if Jackie still got terrible headaches after orgasms. It stirred him a bit to think that the same noise for pleasure and pain had scared him so much at first.

There was no question of Tina being jealous of Jackie. As long as he and his wife weren't fighting he could barely look at her without feeling proud. Sometimes he told her so by bending over and biting her on the bottom, sometimes by handing Anna a note to take to her Mom, a cartoon clipped from somewhere. She would look up and laugh. He needed to spend a certain number of hours a day close to her, and that was what made their love so secure. He would never tell her that he had to stay close because he borrowed her energy. She wouldn't understand that the momentum to roll out of bed in the morning came from her. Or if she did, she'd find it pathetic.

"Do you think," he said, "if I for a minute pretend to agree with your definition of rape . . ."

"Which is," she interrupted, "when a man, any man—friend, lover, husband, stranger, no matter what the external circumstances—puts his penis into a woman's vagina . . ."

"Or any other orifice," he added helpfully.

"When there is even a hint, a murmur, that she may, I say may, not want it there."

"OK. If I go along with that—which I don't . . ." he said.

"You see: a sympathizer." Gordon watched his wife's face. The first time he met her she wore protective eyeglasses and rubber gloves and held an acetylene torch. As an art major at the large state university where he'd gone to get his architecture degree, she'd built metal sculptures the size of large cars. When Tina bent her arm up, the muscle stood up from it like the hump of a dromedary. She was the one who got down under the sink with a wrench and fixed the plumbing. When she hit him, he wanted to curl up on the backseat of his car.

And right now, right now he wished she would cry so that he could take her soft, voluptuous face in his hands and, with his lips pursed for a kiss, blow the tears away. He knew she would eventually manage—see she was doing it now—to pull back and turn whatever it is that makes grown people cry into rage. Tina could stay mad at him for weeks until either he admitted he was wrong (like a priest she would remain open to a change of heart) or he landed a client that would bring them in such a bundle she wouldn't be able to help congratulating him. He fantasized that scenario. This time she'd have to keep her grubby hands off the check.

"I'm not sympathetic to any old rapist," he told her, determined to clear himself. "I'm only saying there's the burden of proof to consider. What about a situation where the man claims—and remember it's just one person's word against another's—that she did say yes and that it wasn't until afterward that she decided she meant no. We're not talking black and white here."

"At least think up your own arguments," she answered. She was referring to the argument that someone else at the dinner party—this lawyer whose name was Laurie—had used.

"Laurie said the victim in the case showed the defendant the birthmark on her upper thigh, and the pink lady even admitted that in front of the jury." As Gordon made this point, he immediately anticipated how she would turn it around.

"That only proves she was telling the truth. Besides, I wouldn't care if she took off all her clothes and boogied for him. She can change her mind at any point. It's still rape." Tina said all this with such righteousness in her voice that it almost didn't matter what words she used. The form of the argument was familiar to him: "I'm right and you're wrong."

"Ditsy or not, Laurie prosecutes these cases every day. And, as she explained to us, the law draws a line." Gordon recognized as he said this that he lacked his wife's conviction. He sounded lawyerlike, Laurie-like.

"Laurie wears a teddy," Tina said.

"Naturally that disqualifies anything she says," Gordon replied quickly.

Gordon stood up, exaggerating his enormous size by stretching on his toes. He walked over to Tina's chest of drawers and opened the top one. There were what looked to him like bits of bark among the soft, lacy, all-white panties and bras. It smelled like pine. He spotted what he wanted and pulled it out.

"Isn't this a teddy?" He jostled it as though urging on a bull.

"It's a camisole. A teddy goes underneath."

"Like a diaper?"

"A polyester-and-lace diaper," she agreed.

"I see. If it were silk, it'd be different?"

"The point is what she called it," Tina explained.

Gordon had seen Jacqueline and Tina exchange disapproving looks every time Laurie opened her mouth. Gordon had to admit that when Laurie mentioned she'd just bought a teddy, he'd gone ahead and pictured her in it. He didn't have a high opinion of Laurie either, but he happened to agree with her equivocal (and for a woman lawyer unexpected) position on rape convictions. At the same time it occurred to him that if he ever decided to become a criminal he'd commit his crimes in the district where Laurie, a blue suit over the teddy, would be prosecuting, for he didn't really see how she could successfully convict anyone of anything.

"I have a solution," he said, and felt pleasure temporarily, like after a good scratch, but as the solution to this whole disagreement flashed through his mind—like stumbling on a checkmate— he heard the blunt sound of a rock hitting the side of their brick house. The middle-class residential neighborhood in the midst of St. Louis reflected the growing pains of the whole country, Gordon had thought proudly when they'd first bought the house that had sheets of cardboard hammered to the insides of all the doors and windows. Like others who had renovated old homes in the neighborhood, Gordon now wished he could transform the character of more than just his own house. The rock was intended for the window, he knew, for he'd replaced the glass in his office only last week. Gordon ran across the hall, opened the window above his desk, and yelled out. He couldn't stick his head out because of the black steel bars that covered this and every other window on all three floors.

Small boys—two, maybe three—ran for cover in and out of the shadows from the street lamps, and he knew from the way they skipped—leisurely, like girls jumping rope—that his voice hadn't scared them. "I'll get you," he hollered, and when he saw a neighbor's face and shoulders in the lighted window across the street he added, "Motherfuckers."

Gordon stopped into the bathroom to take off his pants, and as he walked back into the bedroom wearing his briefs (he normally appeared naked, a big fish to be admired) he thought he heard the bedroom door upstairs close. An image of Jacqueline crouched at the top of the stairs, her little fox face poking between the rungs in the banister, came to him as proof that she hadn't really grown up at all. She'd be able to pretend better if, like him, she had to stay up late reading articles on computer-aided distribution techniques. He'd just won a competitive bid to design a state-of-the art warehouse in New Jersey. When Jacqueline asked what he was working on he knew before saying it that the word *warehouse* would sound so deadly to her, he rose from his seat quickly to stop Anna from putting something in her mouth and said, shrugging, "Stuff."

Tina was leaning back against big yellow pillows on their bed. He had a chance with this new idea to recapture what he liked most in a day, getting in beside her. She'd taken off the lipstick and put something slippery on her face.

"They don't go for the windows in *your* office," he said.

She shrugged. He was glad they hadn't gone for her windows. At night sometimes, after screaming all over the house for him, Tina found him sitting in her office with all the lights out. Draped fabric hung from rods traversing the room, and he answered when pressed that he liked it because he could still dream here. As he spoke he crawled his fingers spiderlike up her dress in the dark, and she squealed not like herself but like he wanted her to. Tina designed prints for fabrics and sold them to cloth makers. The paintings for the designs, frequently fish and fruit motifs, were taped to all the walls. Gordon liked to get close to the part of her that never ran out of these pictures. Without meaning to he interrupted his remembering with an uncomfortable thought: after a while he hadn't been able to make Jackie laugh.

"I think Jacqueline might have been spying on us," he said. He sat down next to Tina on the bed.

Gordon could see Tina running through the things she'd just said, probably wishing, now that she knew Jacqueline might have overheard, that she'd come down harder on her husband.

"You said you had a solution. So what's your solution?" she asked.

If he had presented the idea that had a minute before come to him at the dinner party, earlier, who knows what he and his wife might be doing now. But then he remembered that his wife's responses to his ideas, even to his quips and the ways he phrased things, were unpredictable. For instance, this evening when a guy stole a parking spot from Gordon before the party, he'd rolled down his window and yelled out, "You puckered-red-rosy-rat's-ass." Not, in his view, a clever comment. But Tina had laughed in a big way. Then she'd leaned over and given him a kiss. Maybe it was that his curls were lying just the right way against his neck, maybe he'd put on the right tie, or maybe you puckered-red-rosy-rat's-ass really was funny. Gordon's family was mostly Irish, but when he was young they lived in a lower-middle-class Italian neighborhood outside Chicago. Tina had grown up in the well-to-do suburbs of Detroit. As often happened when he asked what was so funny, she giggled and said she'd just never heard it before.

"OK," he ventured, "Laurie told us that if someone is convicted of rape, he gets ten to thirty years." He paused, meaning for Tina to encourage him to go on. She was supposed to want him to redeem himself.

"Jacqueline thinks you need a vacation. She says she's never seen you so angry."

"Talking about rape makes me angry. Being told I'm angry makes me angry."

"You should tell her your solution too," Tina pleaded, "show her that you don't really think men sometimes have a right."

"So you believe in a solution you haven't heard yet?"

"I'm hopeful," she said, snuggling the pillow.

"All I'm saying is that a guy who was practically seduced . . ."

"Seduced by a birthmark?"

"You can't tell what does what for certain people. Anyway, a guy who's maybe only a touch out of control doesn't deserve thirty years."

"Life. He deserves life."

"Tina. It's not like he did it to her when she was drunk and unconscious. All I'm saying is thirty's too many when we're not sure. The defendant says she only said no afterward."

"So the jury can decide if he's lying."

"But that's been the problem all along. The jury's full of suspicious men like me who maybe don't believe either story. No, my idea is to institute Rape-one and Rape-two. Rape-two would be for all those borderline cases that for one reason or another get dismissed under the present system. So the accused guy in a wishy-washy case is more likely to get some penalty."

"Castration?"

"Calm down mad woman. Save it for the guy who gets convicted of Rape-one. Him I'll let you lock up for good."

"So why were you so piggy at dinner? You said some women want to be raped. You said that and you were staring right at Jacqueline."

Tina got out from under the covers and went walking around the room again.

"I don't know what got into me," he said, but then thought that wasn't quite true. "Jacqueline was pushing my buttons." He said it in a conciliatory voice.

"WHAT BUTTONS?" she screamed so loud that he wondered if he hadn't actually wished for the rock that just then hit the side of the house. Tina had finally reached the point he feared she would: horrible things *had* happened between Gordon and Jacqueline. A moment of silence followed, then they heard scrambling-around noises upstairs. Jacqueline. Would he or Tina run out to see what was going on? He'd gotten angrier about the rock the first time it had happened, therefore he should go. The next rock landed between the iron bars, shattering the window in one instant and in the next bringing all the glass down on top of his desk.

"Oh dear, you should have let them use the hose," Tina said. Gordon meant to ask what she meant, except that Jacqueline, who must have tiptoed down the stairs, was standing at their bedroom door wearing sneakers and Chinese pajamas.

"Hurry," she said, gesturing for Gordon—that was clear—to follow.

By the time Gordon pulled his pants on again, put on shoes, and pummeled his way down the long flight of stairs, stripped by Tina first of carpet and then of paint, and made it through the front door, flung wide open into the now quiet street, Jacqueline was gaining on the two boys.

Gordon sprinted too. After a hundred yards, he stopped and watched Jackie fly on. How had she stayed so fit? The first time he'd heard Jackie cry, she'd grabbed his arms and tossed them, it had been like a toss with those limp arms of his, around herself so that the next time he would know to hug her on his own. Jackie was a thin woman, but he remembered how she once tried to lose weight by eating only carrots for a week and turned pale orange in front of him. He hated the way each time she cursed her face got mean and wrinkled. And there were always used Kleenexes in piles beside her bed. "You should see the way her genitals hang, actually hang, out of her body," he once told Tina, trying to convince her that really what Jacqueline most wanted was to be a man. She'd encouraged him to be outrageous, and then, when outrageous things to do and say started coming to him on his own, she accused him of using what she'd taught him against her. After a while he hadn't always bothered to find out why she was crying. So often she kicked him out of her room before he was ready to go.

Gordon saw the boys split up; they jumped hedges on either side of the road. Jacqueline slowed down and jogged back to Gordon.

"Motherfuckers," she said. "Why do they pick on you?"

Gordon suddenly remembered nodding when a strange boy had come and asked if he could cool off under Gordon's hose. But when he saw five or six black and Hispanic boys join in, he'd changed his mind. He'd offered to give each one a quick dusting off—as though he were washing his car—but he didn't want them dancing in his driveway. He remembered saying something about having to go to the dentist.

"Revenge," Gordon said, turning toward Jackie as they walked slowly back down the dark street. "Something you know something about. You were listening to Tina and me, weren't you?"

"You guys fight like wimps," she said.

"We wouldn't have been fighting at all if it weren't for you."

"If I'd hit you like that—boom—a sledgehammer to the chest, you'd have hit me back."

"I don't hit people," Gordon said.

"You hurt me, you know," Jacqueline said calmly.

"We hurt each other," Gordon replied in a voice that strained for accuracy. "What's the point of bringing all this up fifteen years later. It's as though you're trying to turn Tina against me. I never really did anything to you you didn't want me to, and you know it."

"So I've changed my mind. I wish you'd never touched me."

"And that's supposed to count?"

"I fucking hate men," Jackie said.

It was dark out; if there was a moon it was clouded over. All the light came from unnatural sources, vaguely through curtained windows and from the street lamp many yards away. Gordon couldn't see Jackie's face now because she'd turned from him, but he knew it would be twisted up, as though expressing all the pain she accused him of causing her.

"Tina wants you to be Anna's godmother," he suddenly said.

"And you?" she asked, her voice softening.

Gordon was stuck. To him, the only point in Jackie's favor was that if both he and Tina died, Anna would be glued not to an ostrich or to the doll with the ugly face, but to money. Maybe. Jacqueline was capable of deciding that money screwed children up. She would, after all, know.

"You got lucky, you know. You big slob." Gordon couldn't figure her out. She sounded almost friendly now.

"Lucky?"

"Tina," she explained. "Believe me, you got lucky. She brings out your panda-bear side." Jackie laughed good-naturedly, and Gordon joined her.

"Don't pandas just eat and shit all day long?"

Jackie pointed a finger at him. "You said it, not me."

When they arrived back at the house, Tina came out of the front door. Her mouth opened when she saw Gordon and Jacqueline. She was standing on the stoop, still wearing white, still with her beads on, her pale lips and shiny face, and Gordon guessed, looking at his wife as she came down the steps, that she was seeing for the first time in several months—she forgot things and then got angry about them over and over again—that there were parts to both these people she didn't like.

She led them inside, and when they were in the front room—it was full of cool air, and the colorful walls were lit with halogen lamps—Tina turned to Jackie and said, "Gordon has something he wants to say to you."

Gordon knew Tina expected him to apologize to Jackie about his sinful remark at the party, but he was thinking, so he said nothing. Maybe Jackie was right, maybe it did count that she wished he'd never touched her. He felt the tension between the two of them build. Lately, when he got next to Jacqueline and saw her "don't-dare-bore-me" eyes he wanted to leave the room. But now, as they both stood under Tina's gaze, he saw that whether he walked away or not Jackie would always find a way to get to him. Sure, in a few days she'd be back in New York City, buying low and selling high or whatever else she did with all her time and money, but she wasn't going to let him forget.

"Tina and I want you to be Anna's godmother," he said, and though it wasn't what he wanted at all, he found that saying so was easier than apologizing.

It wasn't until Tina and Jackie each took hold of one of his lumpy hands that he knew he'd given up too much ground. Gingerly, so they wouldn't suspect he was still angry, he pulled his hands away and went to the kitchen to get something to eat. He heard the two women climb the stairs, but stood for a minute longer with his face inside the open refrigerator door, the harsh light illuminating his white, regular features.

Man for Man

The man had become an egg farmer and raised stringy chickens. He lived with pigs and chickens that he tried to keep away from the inside of his home. The pigs had been barred by two wheelbarrow bins wired together, propped up against one corner of the barn. The man probably never noticed the twined-together smells of himself and the animals.

My Lydia knew the man. For several years, many years before, they had lived on the same commune, somewhere in this part of New York State. They had not lived, as Lydia and I did, as lovers, nor even, from what she said, as friends. "The man has no friends," she told me, which was why, I suppose, he used to send Lydia letters, compelling notes, reminders of his unimpressive existence. "The man loved me," Lydia confided, on one of those flashing first days of our friendship. Her feet wiggled impatiently back and forth under the glass coffee table (she had the shapely feet, I soon came to see, of a perfectionist).

Getting out of bed was often the man's task for an entire morning. He tried to remember what was written on his list for that day. If it was chores that could wait, they waited. The lists were more than reminders to wash clothes, to buy chicken feed, to cut wood for the stove, because the lists often mentioned his quest. "Tomorrow I will begin my quest" might be written at the bottom. Or between the reminder to plant Jerusalem artichokes and the reminder to fix the water pump he had written: "Ermine sat on the stool, with her legs crossed, knitting." Often the lists, written on scraps of brown paper bag, changed into passages of prose that were no doubt swept into the garbage and fed to the pigs. Not all of the man's lists, however, were fed to the pigs.

Lydia will not think to look for me on the man's farm. It will not occur to her that his house has become an ideal place for me to hide since he has gone to Africa. She may have guessed that I read her mail, but I don't think she guessed at my interest in the man. Sometimes a month went by before she uttered a detail about that rusted, haunted commune, where some of the freaked-out had gone, where Lydia had gone when she was pregnant with Ziko and full of rebellion against her rich parents. Now and during the time we lived together, she and her mother, in their endless heart-to-hearts over the telephone, confessed regret. I heard only Lydia's side. Traitorous thoughts she had had while living on the commune: longing for silk underwear and Crest toothpaste, hatred for unambitious men, disgust for her pregnancy and the greater pain of a third abortion. Once I heard her tell her mother about being afraid of the man. She never admitted to me that she feared the man. I don't know why anybody would.

Creditors won't find me on the man's farm. A ghastly smell still lingers here. His chickens must have scattered; the corpses of the pigs have dried out. There is no toilet in the house, and he used various corners, mostly in the back room, in place of one, spreading newspaper down on the floor to squat by, not always remembering to pick the newspaper up by the corners and take its contents outside, as must, of course, have been his intention. From his notes and lists, a box of which I have found, along with the information Lydia unknowingly gave, I can see that he was not a stupid man. He must have seemed like a very stupid man.

The man, I know, has a large birthmark from his eyes across his cheek that in the sunlight is a deep red-purple and that his beard, light in both color and abundance, does little to cover. Lydia told me on a sunburnt lazy day together on top of the tarred roof of our New York City apartment building that she tried hard to get over the man's deformity, but could not. When I was a boy, a guy I knew blew off the right side of his face with a

Roman candle. He often caught me staring at the scar tissue. Not everyone understands that to someone like Lydia, who I must admit is something of a beauty with those poised Indian looks, ugliness is unforgivable.

The man had no money. He planned to do carpentry or sheet metal work for a Mr. E. S. Brown, but never did it seems. He planned to do many things. At least he finally managed to get to Africa in the end. He wrote about someone named Ermine over and over again. Ermine, I have deduced, works behind the counter in the Rensselaer Falls Diner, and the man went to the diner every day for tea. He says in one of the notes that he wished he could afford to take meals there. I ate in the diner yesterday, and it was not at all expensive.

> Ermine has never given me one of her hand-knitted scarves.

This sentence appears several times in his note writing and is once followed by a more unusual, rambling sentence:

> While Ermine was sitting on the stool knitting, I thought of how Jake Akenson, a snowmobiler, ran over Ermine's cat with his skidoo eight winters ago and then a month later drove the same monster between barbed wire and might possibly have died of pneumonia, lying all night bleeding in January air; had he died Ermine could have worn her black scarf.

Surely this thought had made the man smile.

On another paper he had written in slightly different handwriting:

> Delivering two grocery bags up Ermine's steps, I tripped, eggs smashed into my elbow. She saw from the window and dared to laugh, knowing me. I am sure my purple mark haunts her the way it did Lydia, who always wanted another life.

He must have stared oddly at Lydia; men do. Even I, who have lived a fortunate life, can imagine what his obsessions cost him. Africa has no doubt saved him! Traveling can.

On corrugated cardboard he has noted:

> Ermine stands by the sink in her house which is neat in comparison to mine, I have only been inside once but have looked through her windows many times. Her hands cup water which she splashes on her face. I imagine telling her she is the veritable love of my life. I am afraid she will say so what. But she just smiles and dries her face with the dish towel making faces at its cast-iron odor.

I have decided to stay in the man's house. If he returns from Africa he will be glad someone made his home habitable. I will spend the next month cleaning up after the man's squalor: dried peas, cornmeal, moldy bread, dirt in the kitchen—not dusty earth, but layers of swelling decay. It will become a place where I do my work. I am an artist and I am ashamed of my life.

During the next few weeks I resurrect the man from the bits of paper that I find scattered all over his farm. The more I read the man's words the more I move toward my own work. Sometimes I fear my art has become an indulgence. I felt so before, which is why I originally decided to engage love with Lydia. Engage is the correct word because I made our love up. I concocted it, pretended it. I had never swooned, and I decided to one day for the sake of my work. I believed then, as strongly as I doubt now, that anything is justified for the sake of art, including someone else's irrevocable pain. The pain will strengthen her, I thought. I do not express myself well, as the man does, evoking himself from nothing.

On the wall beside the place where his bed used to be (I have moved it near the window, turned the mattress over, and of course thrown his old sheets out) there are pencil lines, as if he took a pencil to bed to write but changed his mind. Torment is engraved in dark lines all along his bed. From where I sleep I see leaves glued to the window with rainwater and a collapsed wooden structure already coated with treacherous bits of frost. I have heard the north-country winters are too cold and wonder whether I will stay through the winter.

On certain scraps he jotted images, which unless they have been torn from a larger page of writing are just that. Many of the images do not make sense to me, though most of them I like.

> I see the plain form of dusty white caribou antlers—purple-veined white china hands wearing three gold thread rings.

He may have been writing about Lydia's hands. They are Lydia's hands. But one does not expect the man to write such sentences. There are more of them:

> Sometimes my mind just goes away the way mice do after a night or two of poison traps the way glass-bowl fish die of sudden aloneness.

And on another he recorded an incident that might have ended his voyeurism for a time:

> Through Ermine's window a few years ago, I noticed an owl's wing and an owl's claw, some boy probably gave them to her, on a bookshelf. The bone stuck out from the owl's claw. Had the boy chopped it off the owl or had he found it chopped off? The end where the bone stuck out was a dried scab.

Other scraps are more typical, more what one would expect such a man to write:

> Learn how to take care of the pigs today. Ask P. Wyckoff. P. Wyckoff's sow is as big as a Volkswagen. But all it can do is lie still while four young pigs suck at nipples as long as fingers. Think about trading for a cow: could get my own milk then which would save money and could learn how to make yogurt. Time to plant tomatoes next week I think. Find out when to plant corn. Saturday plant more herbs. The chickens must be sick. Ask vet why they are not laying eggs.

By glancing at the man's garden I saw that he was not a farmer. It is still possible to tell that the herb portion was the most carefully tended. Even it is strangled by weeds. He smoked the herbs and used them for teas as well as for cooking and healing. There are several herb books by the chair in one of the downstairs rooms; it might be his reading room, though there is no light.

I am obsessed with the man's images. They are feeding my work, which I have begun near my reading place. Each day I add several coats of latex to foot-wide panels on his walls. When dry, the hundreds of coats will be ready to peel off and then, then I will hang the strips, which should look almost exactly like human skin, from the rafters. From my intuition of the man, I feel sure that he would be fascinated by my work.

I do not admire the man's slow introverted depression. He was a very lazy man. Without effort toward his quest, he was able to write:

> I am beginning to sense that I will fail in my quest.

This thought appears several more times:

> I now sense that I have failed in my quest. I am convinced. In some non-western countries men are encouraged to have two wives. Ermine, whom I have courted every day in the diner for eight years, is lost to me. Perhaps I should have given her something: a wall hanging of giraffes or a better stool, one with colored beads hammered into the wood, or I might have carved her a chess set though I am sure she does not play or found her a pair of peaking sunglasses, like the movie stars wear, in Ed Iverson's variety store.

The passages of prose, probably after the man senses his loss, become hazier:

> Last night, I dreamed my only dream. It starts with lions chasing me down red corridors. And then I swim, escaping the lions, down rivers, overflowing with rapids, which I, though I do not swim well, have learned to manipulate. For days I swim until I find underwater caverns lined with raspberry bushes where I hide in a submarine forever like saying the world can go to pot as long as I get a raspberry now and then. Tomorrow I will leave the farm. I must leave because I no longer have a reason to be here.

I know that he did not leave the next day because that sentence, too, is written several times.

> Tomorrow I will leave. Monday, after I find a home for the pigs
> and chickens, I will leave. P. Wyckoff might want them. Gray
> boulder nights and misty wheatfield nights. The river which I
> have stood by for so long in snowshoes to watch bits of it
> harden then float away. Crows in the cornfields are blurred
> black things or are funeral people viewed from the branches of
> a chestnut tree. I will also miss watching Ermine fry eggs for the
> customers.

Finally he wrote:

> There is a ship leaving from Machias Port to east Africa at the
> beginning of the month. They need workers or ship hands. I
> have never worked on a ship and hope that I will not get seasick
> before reaching Mombasa. I have decided not to say good-bye
> to Ermine. I will wrap up my jars of herbs and leave them in the
> diner next to the cracked bread box with a note.

Except for the part about Ermine, this was similar to what the man had written to Lydia, similar, that is, to the note I found in Lydia's wicker letter-holder.

Perhaps I, too, should have left Lydia a note. I have not thought much about her. I wearied of her dark beauty quickly, and, after thinking about the man's Ermine, I long for another woman. The wood I have torn from the barn to make furniture with needs sanding. It is the kind of thing Lydia and her daughter, Ziko, might have helped me with, the three of us down on our knees, buffing the smoothed pieces, taking drooling grapefruit breaks, dabbling in arguments about abstract expressionism. Lydia was married to my good friend Alan until I asked her to be my model, knowing how I would pretend to love her and somehow acquire her response. Her love fed my art for almost two years. Now I have the man's words. When my daughter, Malu, was a year old five weeks ago, I left Lydia and, like the man, did not say good-bye, shrouding myself with the delusion that succumbing to profligacy, pinpricking at the brain, is somehow creative. I left

Lydia with the unsold cat tongues. I ordered them from a taxi-dermy catalog. "In formaldehyde under glass," critics wrote, "the 5-inch tongues look like vaginas, penises, and human tongues." Some I dusted with gold and stood up straight, some I left pink, some lay flat and wide open. I rubbed a few with graphite and rolled them. Now I can see the three of them breaking the glass containers with hammers, sweeping the broken bits of my genius into the garbage. Lydia might spit on the fragments or place eggplant skins, which she detests, on top of the mess before letting the garbage truck move my destroyed works away. I want to meet Ermine.

❖   ❖   ❖

Ermine is rather big, too old for my taste and far, far less beautiful than Lydia. The day I entered the diner she was wear-ing farm-girl overalls over a sweeping peasant blouse. She looked as if she would be difficult to rile, calm. Her skin is smooth and good health her most obvious charm. She is in her early thirties, I imagine, probably just a few years younger than the man.

I ordered coffee, and she brought it without milk. When I asked for milk she pointed to it, already on the table. She walked back behind the counter, and I moved up to the counter where the stools were, the same stools the man had seen her perched on, knitting. Ermine's voice was not soft. There was another man in the diner, leaning his elbows on the counter as though accus-tomed to being at the counter talking privately with Ermine.

I listened to the conversation taking place between four elbows as her flat brown hair just about fell in and out of his chili. She found crackers for him and then said out loud, "When things are bad it's always the people on the bottom who get it first."

"Like Bruise-Face," he said.

"I miss serving him tea. Wonder where he went?"

"To Alaska. Everyone goes to Alaska now. Peterson's kid went," the bothersome man said. I wanted to start a conversation with Ermine, so I stared at her by way of the mirror that lined the place halfway. As she turned toward me, I could not help staring at her breasts, bound with a heavy bra, surrounded softly by cotton lace. Not one of my lovers has had breasts of that large sort.

"I'm staying at the man's house." I told her suddenly. "We are old friends," I lied.

Ermine, surprised at this information, went back to whispering with the man now starting on pecan pie. The man eating the pie began the conversation with Ermine. Maybe I have made up his first sentence since it was spoken too softly for me to be sure of it: "I know you could grow a taste for me, Ermine, the way a man does for snuff."

I interrupted their conversation to ask for crackers and then said, point-blank, "You knew the man too, then?"

"Sure. He sat over there." She pointed against the wall. "He sat over there every day and stared at me. Sipped his tea. He didn't like Red Rose much. That's the only kind we have. Red Rose."

"How long had you known him?"

"Nine years. He came from one of those communes and then stayed. Bought the house for nothing and did nothing to it even though he said he was going to. It's a pigsty. The neighbors didn't like him. He smelled and the dogs chased him. Seemed to know, though, which is why he sat over there." Again she pointed to where he had sat. "He had trouble getting things done. Everyone said he was real lazy. But I didn't think that was it. I was the only one to stick up for Bruise-Face."

"He loved you, you know."

"Me?"

"Yes."

"No." She shook her head, charmingly.

The man finishing his pecan pie said, "It's true Ermine. You could tell the way he was shy around you."

Then Ermine said, "I told him not to leave a tip after a year or so. Once he delivered my groceries when the delivery boy got busted. He tripped on the steps. The eggs smashed all over his chest, and I laughed, though of course he didn't see me. He couldn't know people."

Ermine served another piece of pie, and I left the diner knowing that I would stay in the man's house until he returned.

❖   ❖   ❖

I am more capable of living than the man. The kitchen floors and counter are now clean. The smell lingers less each day. I have torn down another part of the barn and burn the decayed pieces in the stove when it is cold at night. The man wrote a lot about the cold.

> Coiling for morning warmth, reluctant to crawl through the bitterness of February air, no one can know how wearily. I dangle a string tying it in bunches with untidy knots, thinking how easy it would be for the chickens under my chair to knock me over. It would take days to recover. I am never rough with Ermine.

I despise the man when he is in that mood.

Ermine, someone I came to know in a way I would never have predicted, made me see that Lydia did not exaggerate the man's ugliness. I believe it is because I am not ugly on the outside, the way he apparently is, that Ermine, to whom I was not the least bit attracted, seduced me. She sought me out, away from the diner. Wearing a tacky waist-length fur—built in pieces, it had a glued-together rat-hide quality—a man's dungarees, and high-heeled boots not high enough to conceal a stocky build, she knocked on my door. His door. The first time I answered immediately, not knowing. Thereafter, when she came, I paused before letting her in. I caressed her cold smooth face as she stood in the open doorway with the dark sky, the shadows of vegetation, and the cruel cold silence framing her. She was so absolutely three-dimensional. As I thought about my predisposition for dainty women, I also thought about the man's desire. He never guessed how cold her skin got or that she smelled of subtle sweets, of the vanilla and strawberry teas she liked to drink. My lust for her came on the way tipsiness finally results from wine. It grew stable only as I raised her heavy nipples with my tongue, thinking, his tongue, his tongue. Understand, I did it for him.

Stubbornness against the world still fastens me to this place. I don't yearn as much to imitate the man's suffering or to fulfill his doubtful quest. I build and tend, bring light into his house through daily gestures: washing windows with heated water, receiving, unasked for, fantastically red curtains from a woman who could not have been persuaded to sew for the man who loved her more, much more—for I do not love Ermine at all. I still sleep with her, as I said, for his sake.

Stone steps, which do not strike me as suburban because I left them shaped like soap chips, meet the front door. And the door shuts properly now, no drafts, no smells. I have installed proper plumbing, and my shaving apparatus sits neatly on a shelf above the sink, beside the dime-store mirror that distorts my face. Ermine was impressed with the toothbrush rack I invented in which toothbrushes lie slotted on their sides.

I cannot believe that the man did not know about the bullfrog pond. I came upon it as I walked beyond the two fields, beyond the Finch boys' tree fort. Once I heard a young girl crying within their wooden castle, and if I imagined young boys taunting or torturing her, which I did, I supposed at the same time that their cruelties were even more advanced and updated than my own.

The bullfrog pond may have been the man's idea of paradise: murky, hidden, hated by the world for being ugly and useless. I will take the man to it the morning he returns, for the frogs are less territorial then. Not many people know that when you are lying back against wet grasses, wearing the thickest possible woodsman sweater, bullfrog songs can be as impressive as a symphony orchestra.

Walking through the fields can make men like me and the man feel almost heroic. The colors are more crowded as each of the seasons repeats, and I see more. In the distance sometimes, depending on the light, many shrubs brush upward off the hillside like—so the man says—the scattered curling hairs on his chest.

His frigid garden yields for me: carrots, onions, corn, marijuana. More delicate plants I cultivate closer to the house, below my bedroom window. The barn, once a burial ground of sorts, is my studio. Although the chicken coop, the side sheds, and the makeshift pigpens are gone, and only the main body of the barn remains, it is still a luxury for me to have a studio that is not at the same time my living quarters, the way it was in New York.

My skins are ready to come off. Tomorrow, I will peel them from the walls. I have changed my mind about nailing them to the rafters. They must hang over the windows and blow fitfully in the breeze.

I have taken to going to the local bar, initially in order to avoid seeing Ermine so often. The repetition of her big-boned, too friendly body bored me. To hear her sleep made me feel mean. I used to let her have his small bed to herself and then went to read in my chair. That hurt her. I know it did because of the way she looked at me as she shook me awake to say she was off. I regretted the mascara dribbling from her eyes and the fact that I did not want to suggest she stay for breakfast. I know, too, because it also used to hurt Lydia when I left our bed and Ermine is more sensitive about such things. Unlike Lydia, she never said a word. Ermine is a good woman. After I made her understand that she could come over once a week or not at all, my reason for going to the bar was simply to relax and have one or two glasses of rye.

The company at the Tick-Tock Bar, just off Route 64 on RR#3, did not exactly please me. It was a men's bar. When I walked in, I saw a pool table, a pinball machine, two wobbly fooseball tables, a dated jukebox, an enormous plastic moose head hanging too close to the ceiling, and men of all ages. Most of the older men had the look of those whose bad ways cannot easily be justified by circumstance.

It was obvious from the moment I came into the bar that I was its most handsome, most worldly client. Their faces were more distorted than mine is when I peer at it, vainly hoping against age, in the warped Woolworths mirror. The immediate and single-minded attentions of the few young women who frequented the bar should be proof of this. Two baby-faced girls, with slightly older complexions, wrinkled polyester dresses, and undeveloped bodies that promised they would sleep like children, winked at me in unison. They sought me out, thoughtfully, as if carefully sifting through men, each time I entered the bar. Although there was also a woman who strolled in a few times and sat by me— a stranger with pointed teeth and a high-fashion widow's peak— I mostly attended Julie and Nancy, sisters, whom one warm night that fall I had the bad judgment to bring back to the man's house.

I will never say exactly what happened with Julie and Nancy, both natural blonds, because I do not want to remember the night and I do not want to disappoint the kind of imagination that would accuse me of atrocities. Even the man might someday judge me, for he had a bothersome tendency to moralize.

Little more went on than smoking the man's marijuana, which he had enjoyed so much. Soon after I came here I came to enjoy it, and the fourteen-year-old Julie and fifteen-year-old Nancy enjoyed it from the start. If I think of it, I can envision the man satisfied with the way the two girls looked. They sat with their little legs dangling off the bench I built from new wood, their plain features softened by smoke clouds as they toked elegantly on his fat pipe. Foremost in my mind is the sight of them sleeping together in my bed, still dressed, still rather coarse-looking, still as sweet a sight as I'd seen since the moths got caught in the oven; I watched them flutter in a panic before they found their way out the oven door I had held down with a brick to ensure their escape.

Having admired the sisters' young beauty the night before, I was not in a mood for Ermine. I refused to speak to her the next day when she came in with the fog. I went from room to room pretending to do certain chores. She followed me.

Finally, my rudeness made her tell the truth.

"The man," she said, with spitting fervor, "is in Ogdensburg, not Africa." When someone has no conceivable reason to be in Ogdensburg, and when Ogdensburg is uttered in a certain contemptuous way, what is being referred to is the Ogdensburg State Mental Institution. She didn't have to explain what she meant about his whereabouts. At that moment, I knew. "He tried to kill himself, you know; he killed the animals," she said, gaining confidence as her news took visible hold of my face.

"You lie," I said to Ermine, who I knew was telling the truth. "You, lie, LIAR," I screamed at this woman who wanted nothing more complicated than comfort.

And she screamed back. "He was a better lover than you are! A better lover," she screamed, thumping her thigh with her fist. I stopped slapping Ermine as soon as I realized she said better lover, not better artist.

She finally left. Because she was crying I never got to say a last kind word to Ermine. I wonder if the man did. A kiss behind the ear? Probably they just came and took him.

I can't work since Ermine left. The skins peeled away beautifully. The color is a little off on the white ones, so I nailed those down on the top and the bottom so that they puff out rather than flap in the wind. I have no new ideas about what I will create next. His footsteps, remember, are mine.

I will go see if what Ermine said about the man is true or at least see how true it is. If he has passed into monotonous territory and if I find him listless, with nurses and a runny nose, and some foul obsession such as repeating certain words or answering the same to different questions, I will pretend not to recognize him.

He tried to kill himself, you know; he killed the animals, she said.

I didn't immediately understand his violent urge, and I thought during the time I screamed at Ermine that no matter what he wrote down, it is impossible to know certain things about anyone's life. But now I picture the helpless pigs and chickens. They squeal. They need food and shelter. When it isn't there, they grow unreliable and mean. The man was afraid he was like the animals. I know. Nonetheless, tomorrow, after I do one or two things around the yard, I will leave the man's house. Tomorrow, I will visit the man in Ogdensburg and we will commiserate over what I have done with his life.

Bold

Unlike Janet, Roz was bold. Roz, with her narrow hips, her appealing little freckled face taken up mostly by a mouth, almost always open as far as Janet could tell. Making oinking noises for Janet's new niece. Sucking up to Janet's mother with some outrageous compliment, "What great feet, doesn't your mother have great feet?" Answering the telephone all week when it wasn't even her house, her loud hello a sort of question, as though expecting this call was going to change her life. Blowing kisses to Janet's brother, Ed, across the TV room. Janet had actually watched her do it.

It seemed to Janet that it wasn't until Roz saw how much she'd embarrassed Ed with her floating valentine (Roz and Ed had been lovers for only two months) that she'd laughed and started telling a story about a retarded boy she used to teach who loved pork chops and who went around asking everyone if he looked good naked. When Roz came to the "do I look good naked?" part, she spoke as though she *was* the retarded boy, naked and with his mouth full of pork chops. As far as Janet could tell, the point of the story was that she related to him and all the other retarded kids in the school where she'd taught briefly, for she, Roz, was always saying or doing the wrong thing; it was this mouth she had. Hadn't Roz slapped their grandmother on the back during Christmas dinner to congratulate her on her new teeth? "Way to go, Gran," she'd said loudly at the table, and Janet's whole family had stared—it wasn't *her* Gran. Right after one of Roz's outbursts, Ed bragged about what a great actress Roz was. "And she writes her own material—amazing stuff."

Janet didn't blame her brother for trying to make Roz's peculiar charm more accessible to his family.

Janet rolled onto her back and looked up at the ceiling of the large house she'd grown up in here in Winnetka, Illinois. Janet and her brother lived in New York City now (so did Roz) and were home for Christmas vacation.

Go. Stand up, she told herself. Instead of moving from her supine position in the hall, Janet moaned and slammed her arm down on the floor. Would Roz ever do what Janet had done? God knows. Maybe Roz would snort wildly when Janet told her, or maybe she would take Janet's hands and whirl her around in a raucous polka. Dizzying. God knows what Roz would do or say. Hell, maybe Janet should give herself credit; for once, *she* had been bold. After an old college professor—"fucking brilliant" was the way she liked to describe him, remembering to add that, oh, yes, way back he'd made a pass at her—had refused to donate his sperm to her so that she could have his child (no strings attached—she had underlined it several times in a PS), Janet had gone to a clinic and gotten inseminated. There: bold.

Janet sat up, then stood. Go. Now. Janet ordered herself into the bathroom next to her brother's old room where her mother had assigned her to sleep this holiday. Instead she leaned over the balcony of the upstairs landing: downstairs, her parents' party had begun.

An hour ago when Janet stood at the island in the kitchen of her parents' suburban home placing canned oysters on melba toast for the New Year's Eve party, Roz had insisted on helping, holding up each oyster and saying who in Janet's family it looked like. Janet wanted to know why Roz had singled her out. "Oh pussy, pussy, pussy my love," Roz had sung absently yesterday as they trudged to the car together in borrowed snow boots. And just look at Roz down there now—you'd think the crowd was full of bigwigs the way she sucked up to everyone.

Janet stepped back from the banister. She had thought the wall hid her.

"*I*," Roz called up to Janet loudly and then stopped. She stood at the bottom of the curving staircase and finished her idea, *"was thinking of a plan, to dye the Janet green."*

And then her brother's girlfriend—this apparently successful performer Janet barely knew—actually began to crawl up the stairs like a caterpillar or like an animal ready to pounce. Where did she get off—acting as though they were best friends with secrets and passwords. *Dye the Janet green?* Janet waited for Roz to rush up the remaining stairs to give her a hug, but another guest opened the door, and Janet's brother called Roz away. Janet watched her exaggerate shaking hands in a businesslike way, up and down violently like a fierce windup toy, as though parodying the custom and those who abided it. All vacation long, Roz had been squeezing the breath out of Janet.

Janet snuck into the bathroom and shut the door. She dug into her purse. It occurred to her as she read the instructions on the side of the box she took out that maybe Roz and her old professor had something in common. Maybe they'd flipped in similar ways—saying things no one could quite get hold of. "Old Fart," she said out loud. His romantic notions about women and motherhood . . . surely they were as outdated as his flabby torso and seedy tweeds.

Arranging herself on the toilet, Janet peed into the plastic cup she'd taken out of the kit. *Women's liberation from Nature has its price.* Where did Charles get off sending her these messages? So what if she'd asked him for his sperm. Her face burned with the embarrassment of having put her request in writing. She didn't have a way with words. If she'd proposed meeting somewhere, at some resort in the Catskills (she'd pay, professors never had any money), she knew he wouldn't have used his intellect to hound her like this. For many years after Janet graduated from the college where Charles taught, they'd exchanged success stories through the mail—the books he'd published, her decision to do an MBA and her starting salary of more than he'd get ever—but she hadn't seen him for ten years. How could she have imagined he would be the same man? What did these notes he kept sending her mean? *Woman squats closer to the earth; she must bear Nature's burden.*

Janet poured the urine she'd produced into cup A and ended the procedure by hiding cup B behind a pack of Kleenex in the medicine chest. She checked the instructions: fifteen minutes for the color stick to turn.

Using the toilet seat as a chair, Janet looked out the window at the driveway banked with snow, full now with Toyotas, Mercedes, Volvos. At breakfast, Janet and her brother volunteered to shovel, and their father had looked up at them surprised: adults now. Janet drew the shade against headlights. It probably hadn't worked anyway. Janet had been to the doctor's office only one time. In and out in five minutes. The doctor smiled, and Janet remembered feeling that she should have gotten to know him better first. It had been such a disappointment afterward, no one to talk to about the dizziness, the uncertainty, anonymous semen dripping onto her underpants. That smell. She'd been told there wouldn't be any, that the massive amounts of semen had been spun down and cleaned, and then what? Put on a For Sale rack, like little envelopes of garden seed. She'd gone right home and taken a bath.

The dripping faucet irritated Janet, but she didn't get up to fix it. Ten days ago when Janet first met Roz, Roz had momentarily pretended to be a normal person and politely asked Janet what she did for a living. She could hear Roz think—BOR-ING—as Janet told her that she was a marketing director for an international consulting firm. What Roz had said to Janet when Janet then tried to explain her job, the slide shows, brochures, and ad campaigns she put together, was, "At least it's free when you get your pap smeared." And Roz had laughed.

"And what do you do?" Janet had asked back. And that's when Janet first heard that Roz was some kind of actress, playwright, sublime artist. Although Janet couldn't get it straight from Roz what she'd written, Ed explained that Roz had just had a one-woman show at the Public Theater. And only two years out of Yale Drama School.

"Don't any of you read the *Times*?" he'd asked.

"You could have called and told me to go to Roz's play," Janet

answered, and Ed looked away as though, Janet thought, remembering there was a reason he hadn't wanted her to see it.
Janet's brother had been in graduate school at NYU for the last
nine years and was, Janet guessed, a good five years younger
than Roz. He and Roz hadn't known each other long when Roz
moved into his apartment in Little Italy, a tiny place with the
bathtub in the kitchen. Roz was romantic about it all, blowing
kisses.

Janet fixed the dripping faucet and sat back down. She pressed
toilet paper against her sweating face, then opened the window
slightly to breathe the cold air. All she wanted now was to regain
the kind of control everyone expected of her. More or less, Janet
liked her job. Boston, San Francisco, New York. At each of the
offices she traveled to, birthdays got celebrated in the conference
room. She knew her coworkers in the New York office found her
overly refined, her white, privileged, Protestant background giving her an advantage she didn't deserve. In a month Janet was
up for another promotion. National head of marketing. Her boss
rewarded her for being . . . consistent. Janet didn't need to hide
from him; brilliant wasn't in his lexicon.

Two years ago she'd had an affair with the firm's maverick, a
Brit she'd gotten to know during his campaign to open an office
in Tokyo. Despite his elevated diction and sophisticated accent
(qualities that had attracted Janet to begin with), he made potty
jokes and rarely picked up the dinner check.

More often, Janet chose men she felt safe with and then grew
bossy. When was the last time she'd lain in bed next to one of her
lovers—how many had there been? forty? maybe more?—and
thought, this is it, I'm happy?

What happened to the French taxicab driver who'd asked her
to have a drink one night? Janet smiled. She'd liked him. He'd
worn lipstick and eye shadow to the Halloween party they'd
gone to together the next night. Yah-net, he said over and over in
his lovely accent, and he'd made her laugh. He told her she was
a passionate woman. She called him on the telephone, sometimes only hours after having said good-bye. And she'd bad-

gered him with questions. "Do you think dreams mean anything?" "Don't you hate politics?" "Does God punish people?"
Always cosmic, never, "What would you like for lunch?" And
then—as always—something went wrong. He lived in a loft
with a bunch of other artists, none of whom would ever succeed
because they never worked on their art. Janet couldn't marry a
layabout, not that he'd even asked. He liked to turn her around
during sex—maybe he'd been gay. Maybe he didn't really want a
passionate woman. Passionate could mean needy.

It'd been five years since she'd heard from him. She used
condoms now. Now, she'd never have gone with him to begin
with. *Bold.* When Charles refused in his haughty tone to be the
sperm donor, Janet called up several friends and began discuss-
ing her other options over the telephone.

Her ex–banker-boyfriend, Tommy Brown, even offered to be
the donor. Around him she'd learned to curse. It was to her
advantage to be able to slap a report down on the conference
table and declare, "This shits." Still, certain words like "slut" and
"cunt" didn't fly with her. Tommy went too far. He was crude.
Janet's friends often told her she was too picky about men.

Screw Tommy. What about her? Maybe she should have given
herself more time to answer a few questions, simple ones like,
what will people say? Or, since when did she like kids so much?

Most mornings as she lay in her apartment back in New York
City on the Upper West Side, three locks on the door, the one on
the bottom opened not with a key but with a tool, with no one
beside her, no one to ask questions of except herself, she forced
herself to get out of bed quickly and shake the questions out of
her head by brushing her teeth—lately she suspected bad breath,
though she couldn't ever smell it—by shampooing her hair, and
then making things whirl—the hair dryer, the teakettle, the blender.
Fed, dressed, groomed, she opened the three locks and closed
them again—it took time—stepped out into the chaos on Broad-
way, made her way to the newsstand, bought a paper, avoided a
succession of bums, then descended the stairs to the subway
platform where she splashed a pool of Coke with her pump.

After being stuffed and zipped inside the train rattling its way downtown, she appeared twenty minutes later up behind a farting, kneeling bus, hurrying her way in the middle of the 8:30 crowd across Seventh Avenue toward her large, windowed office. Questions forgotten.

Wednesday, the week after she'd been to the doctor and the week before she was to leave town to spend Christmas back home, she'd looked up from the newspaper article she was reading while sucking on a lunchtime M&M, and had heart palpitations, perspiration. She closed the door to her office and took off her shoes and panty hose. Feeling better, Janet looked at her calendar. That afternoon, a long meeting with the art department and a list of phone calls to financial planning directors all over the country. Nothing on for the evening. She would stay at work late, go to her exercise class, and then what? Janet flipped to the movie section of the paper. She had to be in Boston by eight the next morning. The palpitations had returned. Janet put her head down on her desk.

Some of the phrases Charles used to use in class—bourgeoisie, ruling class, mindless consumption—came into her head. Charles had practically gotten down on his knees before the students at the small college and begged them to change. Wasn't that what Janet had done when she'd asked him to help her out? Hadn't she broken all sorts of conventions? So why had he been so cruel? Jealous of her salary, only four short of a hundred grand? "Cor-por-a-tion." Janet heard Charles saying the word, a spray of spit landing not so accidentally on the floor.

Maybe she should have stayed out West after college. A fellow ski bum might at least have married her. What was his name, the guy she'd fucked in an empty gondola one morning who'd come to NYC to visit and renew their relationship and she'd been embarrassed by him, the way he'd swaggered down Madison Avenue in a down jacket and construction boots, eating a huge raw carrot he'd bought in a health food store?

Janet stood up and fumbled with a pair of tweezers, her other hand on the sink. Fog spots appeared on the bathroom mirror as she struggled to pluck a blond hair from her chin. Having had lots of lovers—did it really make her different from women who hadn't? Sure, she was at greater risk for cervical cancer. But had all those nights with different men. . . . Janet wanted to know what had made her so dissatisfied. Voices called to her and then faded: take up painting, go to church, double your exercise. She pinched the chin hair again and pulled. Thirty-two years old—maybe time to dump her ponytail. Her friends would be surprised. Of course, having her own child wouldn't solve anything. She didn't expect it to. A long time ago Charles had taught her to read lyric poetry. If she tried hard, she could remember. Rilke: "You must change your life." Unlike Roz, Janet had no artistic impulse. Yesterday, at the car, her sister offered Janet her baby, and Janet had turned away to find something in her purse. Nothing natural about motherhood either.

A loud knock.

"Yoo whoo."

The sound of Roz slurping something from around ice in a glass.

Janet froze, then smiled. Like a child deep into a game of hide-and-seek, maybe she really wanted to be found?

Yet how was she supposed to confide in someone she'd only known—what?—ten days? Roz knew Janet was holding back, and so, like some overzealous lover doomed to fail, Roz kept pursuing her, as though hoarding secrets gave Janet some magical quality the other woman couldn't resist.

"Yoo whoo," Roz repeated. "You're missing your folks' party."

Janet opened the door.

"The woman you just met," Janet said flatly, "she wears that same floor-length kilt every year."

"But *I'm* here," Roz said.

Janet saw Roz turn and knew from the goo-goo look on her face that Ed was coming up the stairs to find them.

"And Ed's here," Roz practically shouted. An actress, mouth open, hip cocked, Roz opened her arms to him.

"Isn't he just the most adorable thing you've ever seen?" Roz asked Janet while she hugged Ed the same way she might easily, and after only ten days' acquaintance, have hugged Janet. Ed rolled his eyes for his sister's benefit and otherwise submitted to Roz's fierce affection.

"God, how do you stand her?" Janet asked her brother. "She's so corny."

"You love it," Roz answered back as she pulled Ed downstairs, her index finger hooked onto the belt loop of his blue jeans.

"I do not." Janet said, more to herself than to Roz, who was gone again.

Foolish to try and correct Roz. Like yesterday when she declared that Janet had to be the sexiest woman on Wall Street when the real picture—the trim suits Janet wore to her midtown office—went zinging through Janet's head. Despite the embarrassment Roz could cause Janet (hadn't she stomped her feet in a little dance when Janet accidentally burped), despite the shivers that spread over Janet's body when Roz appeared in another of her weird thrift-shop outfits, Janet sometimes thought she liked Roz a lot. When Roz walked into the living room, even Janet's mother looked up from her knitting . . . and waited. What will she say next? Who will she make laugh? Still . . . where was it written that Janet had to tell Roz everything? A couple of times, Janet started to, but Roz's intensity—forgetting to blink as she nodded and pried, "yes, yes, go on"—made Janet pull back. What if Roz overreacted? What if she didn't react at all?

Janet sat down on the hall chair and wiped her eyes. She would find her sister Lissa and ask her advice. But Lissa would have to know how it had happened, and for once in her life Janet didn't have a good explanation. How could she be expected to think while Lissa's breasts leaked milk? Right there on her cotton turtleneck, two stains, as though her breasts were alive, salivating.

The pregnancy test. It would be done. Go. Now. Janet stood still, oblivious to her own command.

Janet tightened her leather belt, pinching her waist. She'd dressed down for this suburban crowd. Her brother and sisters and she had grown up here. Her Dad, now a partner in a Chicago real-estate firm that bought and sold skyscrapers, had built all the homes on the lane in the early sixties and sold them for a huge profit. He'd gotten lucky was what she'd decided, seeing no signs in him of killer instinct or business savvy. Didn't her father's generation believe that the name of the game was money? Money. They believed in it the same unquestioning way they believed in God. No one had ever sent her father weird notes he couldn't understand. *In the stone age, man lived in a cave, the womb of the goddess. But now, when man strives to engineer Nature for his own salvation, woman, her womb a cave within, is the last guardian of the mystery.* What on earth? Like . . . women should be eternally pregnant or something?

Janet turned the lights out in Ed's old room and opened the window. Cold air. Being with her family right now made Janet feel lonely . . . and therefore banal. Green? New Year's Eve, the same two men would get drunk. Worse, in a way, the rest of the crowd stayed sober.

Janet put her head out the window and strained to see. Just beyond where the white pines lined up to form a fence at the back of the Nelsons' single acre was the graveyard, beautifully kept with some of the tombstones as big as limousines, others the size of church windows, and still others, Janet thought sadly, small as cinder blocks.

Janet turned. An older man stood alone in the hall downstairs. Just then, just as she was opening her mouth to greet him, her sister Lissa came out of the master bathroom. Saved. Lissa held out her arm for Janet to sniff.

Mom's new perfume?

The sisters stood leaning over the banister together. Growing up, Janet and Lissa shared a large bedroom that had somehow been made small, enclosed by blue furniture, blue carpet, blue spreads, and blue curtains. They used to trade back rubs and gossip about their other sister, Sharon, what a weird bird she was, behind Sharon's back. They were three sisters. Janet still counted her oldest sister, Sharon, even though Sharon was dead.

If Lissa had been the family favorite (over the years, an outburst here, a joke there, seemed to establish this), Janet didn't resent it. Lissa deserved special status. She listened to complaints and made optimistic suggestions—yet there was nothing routine or EST-like about Lissa's positive attitude.

"Is your baby sleeping?" Janet asked Lissa.

"Magic breasts," Lissa answered tugging at her shirt, stained with milk. She'd just nursed her three-month-old girl to sleep. Janet pulled her sleeves down over her hands, making mitts of her cuffs.

"Mom's never put me in Sharon's room before," Lissa commented absently.

"Last night," Janet said, surprised she could eke the conversation forward at all, "I dreamed that Sharon came and stood on a chair beside my bed."

"Sharon's ghost? Here?" Lissa put her hand on her mouth.

"I'm not kidding," Janet continued. "In the dream, Sharon stood over me and was flicking a goddamn drinking glass with her fingernail, and then, like some kind of British actress with a single line, she warned me, 'Her bathtub's always dirty and she's careless in her relationships.'"

The pregnancy test. Why didn't Janet go?

"Maybe Sharon was warning you against Roz. I mean, warning Ed against Roz. After all, you were sleeping in Ed's old room. Maybe you should warn Ed."

"What? I'm supposed to slip him a note that says, 'watch out for Roz—her bathtub's dirty?' Sharon should talk."

Janet had always hated sharing with Sharon. She splashed toothpaste all over the bathroom mirror, left rings of leg hair in the bathtub, the toilet paper hanging down onto the floor. Janet easily wrestled her to the ground, punishment for leaving Janet's bicycle in the rain or for pigging the last three pieces of cake. Sharon had gone through puberty early. Janet remembered coming home from tennis practice or swim team and finding the pile of clothes her mother had washed and folded for her rummaged through. Then later she would see Sharon wearing her shirt in a whole new way, the front undone, nipples poking out like two buttons you wanted to push. Sharon laughing. Janet grabbed her pigtail and pulled.

Later, it became impossible to rile Sharon. Her quiet disdain for Janet's world—television and organized sports—was irritating. Sharon: shrugging, aloof, lovely, messy. In the midst of dutifully copying over her homework, Janet would suddenly stop. What was Sharon doing? And Janet would barge in on her, trying to catch her, doing what? Smoking weed, her feet up on the windowsill. But sometimes Sharon wasn't there. Janet kept checking in on her . . . midnight . . . one . . . two. By five Sharon was usually back, and Janet stood and watched her sleeping face the way she would later study photographs of her. After Sharon's death, once, Janet had gone up on the roof and looked down.

Janet didn't think about Sharon as much as she used to. Sometimes, making love with a man she hadn't known well, she'd pretended she was Sharon, a woman like Sharon, someone a man could idealize, who could idealize a man. It helped take Janet away from fears about whether this man might give her AIDS or she infect him with herpes.

"Speaking of spooky, what do you think of Roz anyway," Lissa asked.

"Roz . . . I kind of like her," Janet answered.

"She came on to me."

"Come on." Janet nudged Lissa, disbelieving.

"I'm serious, she touched my breasts."

"Breast lady," Janet laughed, shaking her head. "Maybe she couldn't help it. I mean, look at you, they're bursting."

Lissa asked, "If Roz's so great, why's Ed still in such a bad mood?"

"Is he?" Janet asked, her own bad mood looming so much larger. "I didn't notice."

"Oh god, there's Roz now. I better save my poor husband."

Janet didn't try to stop Lissa from going downstairs.

Looking down at them all, Janet saw Roz, the big mouth, the cute face with butch hair growing like heavy peach fuzz on top of her head. Maybe it had recently been shaved? Finally, she noticed

Roz was wearing Janet's father's cross-country skiing knickers. No one would believe Roz was visiting her boyfriend's family for the first time.

Through the crowd, Janet heard Roz's odd voice. "Darling." Inappropriately, as though she were mimicking someone with social status.

Had Roz asked her father or had she just gone and plucked his pants from his closet? Janet wondered if her brother had even noticed.

Janet looked at her watch and forced herself back into the bathroom. *Biology hides women's genitals from view.* Charles again. He wouldn't let her open the medicine chest. Had he gone crazy? Why was he going out of his way to hurt her with these notes? She'd left him in the canoe that day, swum ashore. *Spiders, mice, snakes—woman instinctively FEARS foreign elements entering her vagina.* Foreign elements? Spiders, mice, snakes, and . . . a syringe full of anonymous sperm? Was he trying to tell her that she had outraged nature? Maybe she had. So what?

Janet grabbed her purse from the bathroom sink. She'd kept all of Charles's notes. Searching for them she flung glasses and sunglasses, Lifesaver foil, wallet and checkbook, paperback novel, address book aside. The pack bound by a rubber band lay mangled at the bottom, a Jube-Jube stuck to one side. Janet ate it while flipping slowly—no she hadn't dreamed them up.

Aloof . . . like a mannequin in the window of an expensive boutique . . . your uncanny smile when you whisper about your collaboration to trick nature . . . you may still be beautiful but—take note—like Lady Macbeth you are unsexed.

"Too weird," Janet murmured, shuffling the notes nervously. She put them down. This nature crap he was spewing on about, it only referred to her, right? Men were exempt. And if she were married to a man who was infertile, what she had done wouldn't be an issue. Romantic clown. Face it: the world keeps changing, and men and woman will respond separately. She yanked open the medicine chest. And then closed it.

"Anatomy is Destiny." Or it should be. The notes had been with

her for several weeks now, and she was beginning to change her mind about what they meant. Charles wasn't scolding her, he was warning her. His sayings were unequivocal. *Women menstruate and ovulate—they are thus subjects of the moon, lunatics.* Maybe he thought Janet wasn't fit to be a mother. Or that a baby conceived by a single woman in a doctor's office would be deficient. Morally deficient? *Women's liberation from Nature has its price.* Guessing. The way she always had on his exams. She'd worked hard to be one of his top students. Charles . . . remember, he'd propositioned her once.

She paused again at the bathroom door and looked out: her brother Ed's room, cluttered now with her own spread-out things, belts and blouses and socks, the wooden camp bed that her brother's feet had stuck out the end of (Janet had been sleeping in its twin), a cedar chest filled now with their mother's things—family photos maybe and wrapping paper. Her mother's sense of order suddenly intimidated her. Janet wasn't like her mother, not now. How would she explain it if the test was positive? "She'd drunk too much one night, there was this cute guy, and, oh well. . . ." The people downstairs would rather feel sorry for her ("the poor thing," "unwed mother") than perplexed by anything she would do. Artificial insemination. She tried to picture them explaining it to one another: "Janet doesn't like men. . . . No one was ever good enough. . . . She's so independent." "Assholes," she whispered out loud.

Janet ordered herself back into the bathroom. Striding, reaching, her breath wet on the mirror, she yanked open the medicine-chest door. There it was, the little cup full of pee. Strange. Janet lifted the color stick out of the cup, and her face, with no one watching, registered awe, her eyes, blue through contact lenses, taking in everything, a breath of hope in her smile when she saw the rod's blue bloom. Then slowly she reacted. All along, she'd known her body could do this thing. She laughed, as though these secret powers she now knew she had were wicked. Bravado and then despair. Could she possibly keep this child? Downstairs, what would they say?

Standing in the doorway to Ed's old room, Janet felt a cold breeze and went to close the window she'd opened earlier. "Pregnant," she said out loud. "Pregnant," she said again, this time as though the idea were abstract, a concept she was trying out and hadn't quite grasped. The branches of the tree Sharon used to sneak in and out of the house on looked like a poster of a photograph: tree in winter. From higher up in the tree, you could see over the pines into the graveyard. Janet used to love cutting to school through there, closed in and protected, safe. Dead people were dead, she knew. The tree, it's how Sharon had climbed onto the roof that day, the day close to her high school graduation when she'd fallen, or—as the story generally went after traces of LSD were found in her blood—jumped.

Janet lay down on Ed's old bed. Sharon had always had pot. Crammed into one of the upstairs bedrooms with someone assigned as lookout. Lissa liked the social part, bringing them all together. Ed liked the physical—separating the seeds, cleaning the chambers of the pipe. What had Janet liked? Going along, maybe. And Sharon, the oldest, the one no one talked about because she was dead, had been the only one to really love the effect.

Janet had hated the stories Sharon used to tell about her. Like how, from the time Janet was six, she swam in Lake Michigan months before it was warm enough for anyone else. Chop a hole in the ice, Sharon joked; frigid water, Janet loves it. Or the one about how she built a tree fort none of the other neighborhood boys or girls could climb to. Sharon sometimes told people that her younger sister was one of the top woman slalom skiers in the state. And then their mother would add, shaking her head, that Janet's fearlessness would be the end of her. Janet: the rock. Her silly essay in the ninth grade on the virtues of capital punishment. After Sharon's death, no one brought that essay up anymore. Why had Sharon tried to make Janet out as a freak? Tickle her, she won't laugh; just try and make Janet cry, it's impossible.

Sharon would probably have changed. The loose sexiness she'd had as a sixteen year old, a kind of southern drawl to her walk, might have disappeared. Her appetites might have been replaced by ambition. Hadn't her insouciance already begun to slip away? She'd plugged in: the Vietnam War, racial inequality. Janet—forgetting—still thought of her sister as lucky. She'd run free. Men had adored her. Without looking at a photograph, Janet could still envision the blue veins on her sister's neck, her bony knees, the tiny space between her front teeth, her nose—long, overly defined, flared. But more present than any visual memory was the sound of the first shovelful of dirt dropped from above onto Sharon's coffin. Janet had cried, didn't they all see?

❖   ❖   ❖

Apart from the crowd, Janet and her sister Lissa sat in their old bedroom upstairs, now their mother's sewing and hobby room, though it still wore the blue wallpaper. Janet found her mother's hobby sad. The huge dollhouse filled with precious pieces of furniture, decorated with hooked rugs, porcelain vases, real coats hanging in the closets, little cauliflowers and Coke bottles in the refrigerator, working faucets, fresh linens in the linen closet folded like the extra towels in the master bathroom with the rounded edges showing, Johnny-jump-ups—real ones—in boxes around the porch, and, this was the touch that really got to Janet, something she and Lissa had just now discovered for the first time, a miniature picture of the family, all four children in front of the fireplace, framed, over the mantelpiece.

"Is Mom losing it?" Janet asked Lissa as they passed the family photo back and forth.

"Oh leave her alone, it's harmless," Lissa said.

"So here's the thing," Janet said nervously. Lissa's hands lay in her lap. "Remember Charles?"

"The college professor who published a poem about you. Pining, wasn't he? Why don't women ever write poems pining for men?"

"Maybe they do," Janet answered, trying to think. She'd stopped reading poems when she left college. Charles had told her there were two kinds of people—those with literary ability and those without. Janet hadn't wanted him to discover that, on closer scrutiny, she might be one of the ones without.

"He was fat, wasn't he? Not that that matters, but there's a limit, right?" Lissa's arms went wide, deciding.

"I asked him for his sperm," Janet told her sister.

"His sperm," Lissa repeated flatly. "Like in a jar . . . to look at."

"Seriously. I always thought he represented something . . . something, I don't know . . . elevated."

"Are you losing it is more like it. I mean, forget about marriage, Jesus, shouldn't you at least be attracted to the guy?"

"Guy? Guy?" Roz's grinning face appeared in the gap; they should have closed the door. "You didn't tell me about any guy," Roz accused Janet, giving Janet's arm a feverish squeeze as she sat down next to her on the upholstered love seat. "Do you mind if I come in? Everyone is acting so weird downstairs," Roz laughed, nervously. "Ed's barely talking to me."

"Maybe he's pissed because you're wearing his father's pants," Janet suggested.

Roz looked down at her pants.

Janet looked at Lissa and rolled her eyes.

"Hey, don't do that." Roz put her hands over her face, and Janet thought Roz was going to cry. She shook her head as though shaking hair she didn't have from her face and held her head up again—no tears. "I mean it's not easy. Everyone's so wonderful. You have such a beautiful family," she said, lowering her head again. "But it's not easy for an outsider. Nobody talks about it."

"That's right," Lissa said, "Nobody talks about it."

"Three inches, maybe four," Janet reported on the snow from her place at the window. Janet wondered what kind of failed family Roz had come from that made her so want to be a part of this one.

"Guy?" Roz whispered, slyly bringing the conversation back. "Guy?" she repeated more excitedly, seeing the sisters relax a little.

"Oh just some dumb guy," Janet said. Her legs went weak and her throat filled up again, knowing she would soon be coaxed into telling. Then she could admit that she'd probably made a horrible mistake. Roz could be the one to suggest a way out— ABORTION. *Medusa, only with the snakes swarming at your crotch.* How had she ever imagined she could keep this child? Janet turned away from the window where if someone had been standing that day they would have seen Sharon's body falling onto the cement stoop below.

Janet looked at Roz and shivered. What was it about Roz that drew Janet and then almost immediately repulsed her?

Janet walked over to the bed she'd slept in as a teenager and sat down. Janet's mother had taken over this room, but she'd left certain things intact. Janet's crutches from a broken leg were in the closet, and the family's athletic trophies were still on the shelves where Janet's and Lissa's books used to be. Most of the trophies were Janet's. When there were a lot of kids in a family there was no way out, you got pigeonholed: Lissa the beauty, Janet the athlete, Ed the brain, and Sharon, what had she been? drug crazed, now dead. Doctor Doolittle, the complete set, was still there on the top shelf.

"I can take a hint, you know," Roz said. Having waited through Janet's silence long enough, she stood.

"Oh stay," Janet said. "It's just hard for me to say."

"Let me guess," Roz offered. "You're pregnant?" And then she squealed and got all red in the face, and Janet wondered what their grandmother would say if Ed ended up marrying this woman and she became a Nelson too. Roz gave Janet a big congratulatory hug.

"OK. I'm pregnant," Janet admitted. She turned away, afraid to confront Roz.

"You are?" Lissa asked. "I thought you said you asked Charles for his sperm, not that he'd actually given it to you."

"I got someone else's."

"Whose?" Lissa asked.

Janet stared ahead.

"The guy," Roz screamed out. "The just-some-dumb-guy you were telling us about."

"He's not supposed to be dumb. They screen them," Janet said, toughening.

"Your Granny?" Roz gasped, putting her hand to her mouth, startling the sisters. "What will she say? You know, you can make a case for its not being a bastard. I'm sure you have to screw someone to produce a bastard."

"Bastard?" Lissa objected, twisting up her face in strong disagreement. "No one says bastard anymore."

"Bastard," Roz contradicted.

Janet had received the catalog from the sperm bank and gone over it carefully, then contacted a doctor on Lexington Avenue who claimed to know all his donors personally. They were his medical students.

"When is it due?" Roz asked. She stood up and was quivering with excitement.

"Roz," Lissa said calmly, "you're standing so close to Janet. I mean, shouldn't you give her a little more room?"

"For what?" Roz lifted her arms to show she wasn't interfering with Janet's space.

"That's OK," Janet said, sitting, out of range now.

"January, February, March . . ." Roz started counting months on her fingers.

"I'm having second thoughts," Janet interrupted her. "That's what you don't understand."

No one said anything for several minutes.

"I'm not sure I can handle it," Janet pleaded with them. Her sister, even Roz—they were supposed to help.

"Have you ever . . . ?" Roz pressed.

"Ever what?" Janet asked.

Roz drew in her cheeks and made a loud sucking noise.

"Disgusting," Lissa said.

"I've had two," Roz said, holding up two fingers to make the information more tangible. "The paisley buggers swam right through my diaphragm."

"You're a big help," Lissa said softly, countering Roz's hyped-up voice with calm. And then she turned to Janet. "You can't," she squeaked, a shrill sound for Lissa. "You can't just get rid of it."

"We're being too judgmental," Roz said, suddenly protective. "Look at her, she's dizzy."

"I'm scared," Janet said, panicking again.

"Scared," Roz said. "That means you're alive. Personally, I think you did the right thing, facing it—there aren't enough men to go around."

"There're lots of men," Lissa said. "Janet could have anyone she wanted."

"Not true," Janet answered, shaking her head. "I'm sick of complaining about men. I've known plenty of interesting men. I've had my share of lovers."

Roz asked, "Did you see the guy?"

"They make sure you don't. They freeze it."

"What do you know about him?"

"He's cute. That's what the nurse said." Janet shrugged. "Cute?" Roz repeated, as though Janet were crazy. "I'm cute. And I bet you wouldn't want to reproduce me." Roz went and sat beside Janet.

"And tall. I picked tall."

"And white," Lissa added. "You picked white?" Lissa looked at Janet closely. Janet felt her scrutiny: why on earth would anyone do what Janet had? "I have to go to bed soon," Lissa told them, pausing. "But I'm wondering, how will you take care of it? I'm having a hard time with mine, and there are two of us."

"Easy," Janet answered. "Hire someone."

"Money," Roz said, in such a way that she was also saying, see, I told you, money.

"You're both acting as though I'd decided," Janet said. "The thing is, I don't know anymore."

Janet sighed heavily, and Roz and Lissa turned to her sympathetically.

"I know it's taboo, but can I?" Roz asked excitedly.

"Can you what?" Lissa asked back.

"Ask a question? About Sharon? I guess what I'm trying to say is that I took LSD. So did almost everyone I know. None of us jumped off any roof." Without waiting for a reaction, she plunged on. "Is she there?" Roz asked, butting her head toward the window, toward the graveyard.

Looking at Roz, looking inside her open mouth as Roz came to understand that yes, of course Sharon was buried there, Janet, who followed the bobbing, open-mouthed head of the other woman, suddenly thought of her sister Sharon as she had come into the kitchen one morning after a night on the beach with Billy Oluf, guitarist for a local group: barefoot, her separated hair full of knots, her lips plump with blood, her cheeks on fire, and that smell—camp smoke and sex—laughing. Her head moved up and down as it had when she stood on the chair in Janet's dream last night trying to tell Janet something over and over again.

"You know," Roz said abruptly, "the play I wrote, the one Ed keeps telling everyone about . . . the main character is this woman . . ."

"Yes . . ." Janet interrupted, waiting to see what this had to do with her own situation.

"It's pretty horrible . . . what happens to her. I wrote, directed, and acted all the parts myself."

"What happens to her?" Lissa asked.

"It was incredibly controversial. Mixed reviews. I'll never get an NEA. Your brother came only once. He likes the idea of my getting a lot of attention. The truth is," she continued, her hands cupping her mouth, "that my work gives him nightmares."

"Can you tell us what happens?" Lissa asked.

"Well . . . I could . . . no . . . show you."

"Right here," Lissa said. "To give us the flavor."

"Are you sure you want me to?" Roz asked, her whole body quivering with excitement.

Janet and Lissa nodded.

Roz turned out the lights, and the two sisters remained seated in the dark while they listened to Roz rummage around.

"When does it start?" Lissa asked.

No answer. A few minutes went by.

"Hey," Janet said, impatient.

No answer.

Lissa got up, stumbling over Roz's body on the floor, and turned on the lights. Janet couldn't believe what she saw. She flushed.

Roz lay naked on the floor playing dead. But that wasn't all. She had her neck cocked back and a lipstick line drawn across it as though trying to depict a tender white neck that had been sliced like a loaf of bread. Or snapped. Murder? Rape? If Janet knew, she might have gasped and then asked Roz, "What on earth?" But there was more. Roz had one arm wrapped impossibly over her large breasts, flattening them, and then stretched halfway around her back; the hand of the other was imbedded between her legs, two fingers, it looked like, right up inside her vagina. Why? She'd stuffed a fistful of dollar bills into her mouth. For what seemed to Janet a long time, Roz lay there, convincingly dead. At first the sisters said nothing.

"That's supposed to be some sort of a statement?" Lissa finally asked, incredulous. "About what?" Lissa was furious. Roz stood up and started to get dressed.

"No wonder Ed didn't go back," Janet said, her hand still over her mouth. What was Roz getting at? "You did that in public?"

"About yourself," Lissa declared.

"No comment from the artist," Janet remarked to her sister.

"You said you were scared," Roz answered, stepping back into the unflattering knickers.

"So . . . what are you saying? Who do you think you are?" Janet asked.

"Oh god, forget about it. I mean, maybe all I'm saying is that most of us don't see things. Or don't want to look." Roz pulled her shirt over her head and then positioned her hands like blinders on the sides of her face. She took several large steps across the room.

As far as Janet was concerned, Roz had it wrong. For one thing,

Janet had gotten there first, and so she knew Sharon had her clothes on, even her boots. Her head wasn't sliced or snapped, her face was composed, bloated, mouth closed, the three freckles lined up on her nose as always. Her summer arms, Janet thought looking out into the snow, were up as though at the height of forming an angel. Her legs, bent all funny, were those of a hurdler midjump. And there was no money in her mouth, for Christ's sake, just hair. She'd swallowed a piece of her own fragrant black hair.

Roz's exhibition was just an idea about Sharon's death. Abstract, like Charles's notes. Those wordy images of woman he'd sculpted for himself, they had nothing to do with her. Charles and Roz made things up. They depended on drama, and, if need be, they pushed buttons to make it happen. Sharon raped and gored by capitalism? The Goddess Nature imposing her indomitable will on women's bodies? Roz and Charles reaching far afield to avoid their own lives.

Sharon had loved life. Janet smiled, her hand resting briefly, self-consciously, on the spot below her stomach. Yes. For now she knew. She'd always known of course. Sharon used the roof all the time, in and out of Ed's bedroom window. It had rained that day, a Saturday. The roof had been slippery. Janet's mother had closed and locked Ed's window between the time Sharon had gone out and the time she'd come back. Finding it locked, Sharon must have tried to climb around to her own window. The roof was steeper on that side. She'd simply slipped.

"So what will you do?" Roz asked.

Janet wanted to smudge the pink line that still circled Roz's throat. Sharon's neck had been much longer, more graceful.

Janet lied fluently to Roz, "I don't know. I don't know what I'm going to do."

"I think you already chose," Lissa said, clearly.

"So choose again," Roz contradicted, and Janet stared back at Roz until Roz broke away.

"Happy New Year," Roz suddenly screamed, standing. It wasn't midnight yet, but Janet could see that Roz was through with her for now. After all, there was a party downstairs.

Acknowledgments

I want to acknowledge the support of friends and family over the long time during which I wrote the stories that make up this volume. My brother, Kirk, and sister, Meg, have taken more than a passing interest; my parents sustained their faith. My friends Julie Westcott, Allyn Chandler, Judith Belzer, and Stephanie Gunn over the years asked to read my stories and then said wildly encouraging things. So did Jason Bell and Susan Winter. Tony Winner read many of these stories in draft and gave me invaluable advice. Michael Pollan read my work with sympathy and intelligence. Thanks too to my friends in and around Miran Forest: you were the book's first readers, long before it deserved to be one. The Virginia Council for the Arts has at crucial times given me financial support, and for that I'm very grateful. The birth of my two boys, Matthew and William, protracted the project and enhanced it many times over.

An earlier version of "Man for Man" appeared in the Winter 1985 issue of *Sou'Wester*; an early version of "About Johanna" appeared in the Fall 1986 issue of *Carolina Quarterly*; "Generations" was first published in the Fall 1990 (vol. 12, no. 4) issue of the *Kenyon Review*; and "A Leap of Faith" first appeared in the Spring/Summer 1990 issue of *Iris*. The author gratefully acknowledges permission to reprint.